Ted

I hope this book doesn't
kill you too often...

♡ margaret

BEING AN ADVENTURE OF YOUR OWN CHOOSING

# WHAT LIES BENEATH THE CLOCK TOWER

# MARGARET KILLJOY

## ART BY JUAN NAVARRO

I hope this book doesn't
kill you too often —

Margot

*What Lies Beneath The Clock Tower:*
*Being An Adventure Of Your Own Choosing*
Margaret Killjoy, 2011


ISBN-13: 978-0-983497-10-3

This edition published by Combustion Books:
www.combustionbooks.org
info@combustionbooks.org


Margaret Killjoy's website is: WWW.BIRDSBEFORETHESTORM.NET
Art by Juan Navarro: FWACATA.COM


fonts used:
Tw Cen MT
Adobe Garamond Pro
DETECTIVES INC


Printed in Canada on acid-free, recycled paper with soy-based ink.

Never again will a single story be
told as though it's the only one.
                                    —John Berger


There can never be a single story.
There are only ways of seeing.
                                    —Arundhati Roy

## Introduction

Goodly reader, in this story you will take the role of Gregory, a curious and youthful gentleman of British birth living in an ambiguous city in 19th century France. And while this story is indeed adventurous—lest its very subtitle be criminally misleading!—you must bear in mind that you, Gregory, are more acquainted with absinthe and vice than firearms and acrobatics.

But you will not venture forth with empty hands or pockets; we shall not allow you to be so underprepared! At the beginning of this tale you are wearing a fashionable, if cheap, suit—complete with black wool overcoat and starched-felt bowler. You have a pocket watch on a chain. But this is no ordinary pocket watch; this pocket watch has been over-wound and is in need of repair. Your wallet is empty of money; they seem to have taken it all at the bar. In one hand you bear a simple, bronze-headed cane of stained wood, born as an affectation. In your trousers pocket you have a silver ring that you won in a game of chance, a ring that you were hoping to give to your lover. And of course, you would not consider leaving your chamber without an ample supply of intoxicants, which may be found in various flasks and bottles upon your person. It is with these provisions that you begin your absinthe-muddled journey into the depths of the undercity.

This book, as you may have conjectured, does not read like a normal book. This book is not constrained by the limits of linear form. You will be allowed to make choices. Each section is numbered. At the end of each section, you will be either told which section to read next, or be given a choice. Each choice will be presented as a section number, **in bold**, and a page number (in parenthesis). Drunk on the green fairy you may be, we hope that this does not overtax you!

I won't lie to you; some of the choices may very well lead to your death—or to fates still worse! The honest thing to do, of course, when you reach such an end would be to admit defeat. However, it is important to remember that this is just a book. There will be no one to scold you if you backtrack through time and make new, hopefully wiser decisions.

*To begin, turn to* **One** *(page 2).*

## One

The clock tower above your apartment tolls, ringing twice. You sit in your bedroom, which serves as your salon, which serves as your dining room and kitchen, which serves, quite unfortunately, as your water closet. The rain is pooling on the floor by the leaky window, and the wind is rushing through the alley outside with such force that your meager curtains billow and sway.

The green-tinted bottle lies empty at your tired feet, but you are not prepared to sleep. There are letters unanswered, and what sort of gentleman would you be if you delayed in your correspondence?

After the tolling of the bells, you hear a most curious sound, a sound quite unfamiliar to you. It is the sound of an iron gate perhaps, scraping and squealing from disuse. Or it is the sound of a dozen dogs of hell, scratching their claws of steel on the stone of their prison, howling towards the setting moon. But one thing is certain of the noise: it came from the stairwell right outside your door.

*To refuse to investigate, passing it off as the fancy of your tired mind, go to* **Two** *(page 3).*

*To rise, don coat, hat, and cane, and step out of your parlor to see what is the trouble, go to* **Three** *(page 3).*

## Two

You turn your eyes back to the letter before you, but your mind refuses to follow. Untamed, it thinks only of the gateway to hell that must surely have opened so close at hand, setting un-imaginable beasts into the mortal realm. You turn the letter to your lover into a macabre poetry, one that references demons you did not realize you put stock in. The letter to your pa-tron—as the middle-class banker who pays your rent would like to consider himself—is woefully incoherent, and is certain to convince him of your madness.

The wind and rain fall silent, and your room has never felt so ominous. The simple lock on the door suddenly seems inad-equate, and—as much as you hate to admit it—you begin to question your own courage. You wish another soul were present in the room with you, for even the devils of the ninth hell may seem bearable when you've a friend.

*To return to your bed and seek the solace of your ratted down comforter, lighting every lamp and praying to the God whose exis-tence you have forsworn, go to* **Four** *(page 4).*

*To dress and venture into the hallway, facing what you hope to be imaginary fear, go to* **Three** *(page 3).*

## Three

The lamp seems to be out, and the stairwell is dark but for the orange glow that seeps in from the streetlights outside. You pause, letting your eyes adjust to the darkness, and close your door quietly behind you, locking it.

At the base of the steps, a floor below you, lies a dark bundle. To your mind it may be a rucksack, or a child. An imp, or a pile of laundry. It does not move.

Coming from the belfry upstairs, you hear the unmistakable sound of conflict: heavy breathing and boots clacking on the hardwood. Or perhaps it is the dancing of cloven-hoofed demons?

*To venture upstairs into the belfry, go to* **Five** *(page 5).*

*To inspect the bundle at the base of the steps, go to* **Six** *(page 7).*

### Four

An hour passes, an hour during which every howl of wind seems to be the wailing of a banshee, an hour that seems interminable. Eventually, after you've calmed yourself with brandy and lie in a drunken near-slumber, the bells above chime thrice. On the third bell, you hear the noise once more. This must be the closing of the door, you rationalize, and soon you pass into dreamless sleep.

The next noon you awake, your head set afire by the toxins of vice, your palms bearing clear marks where your nails had dug in. You don your hat and begin to walk to the library. You need a book to read, to be certain, but not this one.

### The End

## Five

You make your way up the steps, placing your feet near the walls to minimize the creak of the wood, your cane held at your side as a cudgel. Three flights up you walk, past stained-glass windows of undecipherable biblical scenes. The occasional squeak or scratch you make is drowned out by the cacophony of footsteps above.

Light filters down the steps from the doorless archway at the top of the stairs. When you reach the belfry, you rub your eyes in disbelief. Certainly, you assure yourself, it is some trick of the wormwood, and the small, green figures before you simply do not exist.

But there they are. The belfry is filled with goblins, their long rabbit ears hanging back over their heads, or cocked to strange angles, projecting through their black leather or felt caps. There must be dozens of them filling the small room, each with a unique patchwork outfit; some seem to be workmen and workwomen—perhaps they would be best known simply as workgoblins—in sturdy, functional coveralls, while others are a bizarre parody of your own suited attire, complete with bowler or top hat.

Yet while they dangle from rafters with ruler and knife, examine the bells with tuning fork and soundhorn, and scurry about with clipboard and blueprint, they do not appear to be in the process of repairing or maintaining the bell-tower at all. Instead, they appear to constructing some device of their own. It is obvious they have just begun, yet already they have arranged the metal skeleton of some unfathomable machine.

As you gape, you hear a high-pitched voice, speaking clear but accented English. "Pardon, sir, but you might want to wipe your chin."

"I'm sorry?" you ask, and look about confused. You look down and see a clipboard-wielding goblin, who reaches hardly to your knee, offering up a handkerchief.

"Your chin. You seem to have leaked. I think if you kept your mouth closed, or perhaps open a bit less wide?"

Confused, you take the proffered kerchief and wipe your face.

*To speak courteously to the goblin, and inquire as to their behavior, go to* **Nine** *(page 13).*

*To represent your landlord's interests, demanding that they cease all construction, go to* **Ten** *(page 15).*

### Six

You creep down the steps, one hand on the banister and the other on your cane. When you reach the ground floor, you realize that the stone staircase has a quite unnatural door set into it that you don't for the life of you remember, one that gapes darkness and seems sized for but a child.

And on closer inspection, you realize that the bundle on the floor is not a bundle at all, but is instead a miniature green man. One with long, floppy ears and tufts of white hair protruding at all angles from his wrinkled scalp. You stare, presuming the prone figure to be asleep or unconscious, until you realize that he stares right back at you, his eyelids open a slit to reveal dark eyes.

"Come no closer, gnome," you say, holding your cane before you as though it alone would hold back demons from the nethers.

But as soon as he hears your words, the creature springs forward, lunging towards you and… and crawls between your legs to cower behind you.

"Where?" he asks in a frightened voice. "Where are the gnomes? I cannot see them."

Something in his demeanor—perhaps it is his obvious fear that outweighs even your own—puts you at ease and you shake your legs free of him. "I, well… I thought *you* were a gnome."

"Of course not! I take offense to such comments."

"And you are…" you question the man whose eyes meet your kneecaps.

"A'gog" he replies, walking slowly up a few steps before turning and facing you at belt-level.

"Fascinating," you reply, because you've never before met such a lucid creature while dreaming. "I've never even heard of a gog. Where do gog's come from?"

The olive-green fellow jumps up and stamps his feet on the step. "My *name* is A'gog. A'gog the goblin. I am a goblin, and like any goblin from the undercity, the gnomes are my sworn enemies." A wistful look finds its way into A'gog's eye and he begins to head off on a tangent. "Well, not that the gnomes *know* we are their sworn enemies. They just think that we work for them. Now, a few couple generations back, in my grand-goblin's time…"

You stare at him, curious, but he seems to have lost his train of thought.

"Well then, A'gog. My name is Gregory, and I'm the care-taker of this tower." This last bit isn't the sort of truth you'd really want to call *truth* per se. "I admit I'm rather quite curious what you're doing here, where this door came from, and what the racket above our heads is all about."

"And right you would be to be curious! There's great work afoot, great work indeed!" A'gog comes down from his perch and circles you six times clockwise then six times counterclockwise.

"I've spelled you good. You are now obliged to take hand in our rescue."

"Am I really?" you ask, because you're not certain you believe him.

"Yes, of course. It's one of those *geas* curse magic spells that you humans believe in. It's where I trick you into thinking that if you don't come and do some task, what probably with some kind of shiny reward, you'll turn into a goose and be eaten by your fellows. So then, into the underworld! Us goblins need your help!"

"And if I don't help?"

"Well then, my magic curse will turn you into a goose in three days time, that's what'll happen to you."

"Will it really?"

"No."

You sit down on the stones and pull a flask from your hatband. Sipping on spirits usually does you a bit of good in these sorts of situations. Well, you've never been in *quite* this sort of situation, but it turns out that the gin does, indeed, help.

"Spare a swallow of that for an old goblin?" A'gog asks, and you pass him the flask.

"So well, maybe you're not cursed or geased or liable to get goosed. But see I'll lay it out plain as a planet: we goblins got it bad, real bad. Us and the kabouters—big blind fellows with pasty-white skin and a screech like a bat, you'd like 'em—we ain't been treated like we deserve to be treated. The gnomes have us at lightriflepoint, they do. I'd rather be dead, I figure.

"We've got plans, real good ones and real big ones, to be free. I can't say as I know you enough to trust you with the real working going on above our heads though. But we're building stuff that'll help. Weapons, let's say. And I thought

I'd come with, but of course I decided to take a nap down here since I was getting sorta tired, and now they've all gone ahead and started without me and I don't really have a role in this no more. I'm going to go back through that doorway into a dark world of violence, death, and steam-powered contraptions. You can either come with me—be a hero, or at least another fellow with a good-sized stick—or you can go back up into your little room up there and do whatever it is you were doing with your life, and I promise you you'll never have another chance to see a world aside from your own."

The goblin burps, then giggles, yellow sharp teeth protruding from black gums. The laughter sets him off hiccupping, and eventually he falls over on his side in chuckles.

*To join the goblin on an adventure, go to* **Seven** *(page 10).*

*To return to your room and your unfinished letters, go to* **Eight** *(page 12).*

### Seven

"Right then, geese or no geese, I'll follow you into the dark nethers. I have just one question for you, first."

"What's that?" A'gog asks, calming down from his laughter, but still hiccupping.

"Am I hallucinating this?"

"No, I don't figure you are."

"But you're so short, and green, and well–" you search for the right word.

"Hallucinatey?"

"That'll do."

"Well I suppose *I* think I've been around for decades now, being a rather old goblin. But if I was a product of your imagination, would I know it?"

"I don't know."

"Well, I'm glad that's settled," A'gog says, as if anything were settled.

He leads you into the doorway and down a steep flight of rather obnoxiously short and tightly-packed stairs. Of course, you can't see a thing, but years of stumbling home blind-drunk have taught you a thing or two about feeling your way across treacherous terrain without the use of your eyes.

In fact, you only stumble forward into your guide once during the course of the whole fifteen minute descent.

Eventually, you find yourself in a reasonably well-lit service tunnel that, while tall enough to accommodate you, is packed with tubes, pipes, and apparatus.

"Which way?" you ask, because A'gog has stopped.

"Heavens if I know," he says. "I guess it depends on what you want to do."

And you had presumed that he had some sort of plan for you.

"Well, I think you've got three options. There's us goblins, and we mostly live over that way, in Haddlelint. We're like slaves, and we mine stuff. We also engineer and invent and do all sorts of things that gnomes don't think we know how to, but mostly we just mine. We're staging an attack, too.

"Then you've got the kabouters, over in Underburg—now that's not what they call it, but it's what we like to call it. The kabouters they're like... I don't know what you call 'em up there, but you know, what do you call a snotty fellow who lives outside the city in a fancy little town and has a bit more money than the factory workers but still doesn't have any say in how anything works?"

"A sod," you offer.

"Yeah, that's them. Most of them don't even know they're slaves. You could go there, talk some sense into them. You'd at least get to eat better. Either way would help us, I suppose. Both ways you're liable to end up killed."

"You said you thought I had three options?"

"Oh, right. Well, you could just walk right up to the gnomes in Hak'kal, their metropolis. But you don't want to do that. Forget I brought it up."

*To express interest in Haddlelint and the goblins, go to* **Thirteen** *(page 19).*

*To ask to be taken to Underburg and speak with the kabouters, go to* **Seventeen** *(page 26).*

*To insist that you be shown the way to Hak'kal, to see the gnomes firsthand, go to* **Fifteen** *(page 22).*

### Eight

You take your flask back from your quickly inebriated friend, get to your feet, doff your cap, and return to your chamber without saying goodbye to the hallucinatory little fellow. The storm outside seems to have subsided, and you sit down before your desk, anxious to get on with whatever it is you were doing.

But there, sitting on your desk, is a nether-demon of insufferable agony, poorly disguised as a household cat. It looks up at you, its white fur glistening, and you realize it must have snuck in the window.

"Well aren't you an insufferable bore?" the demon asks.

"Well you see, I couldn't go and have an adventure," you

defend yourself. "These letters, I am behind on my correspondence. What would my friends think?"

"I thought better of you, dear reader," the furious-hell-beast says calmly. "You don't deserve to read this book."

The fiend of the underworld transforms into a hideous manticore—which is just some ugly mix-match of annoying animals like humans and lions and scorpions—and kills you in a rather painful way, one that honestly you probably wouldn't want to hear about. You see, if I told you how it was that you were killed, you might, I don't know, have a sense of adventure. And clearly, that isn't what you want. So you're just dead.

**The End**

**Nine**

"My good sir goblin," you begin.

"Please, call me Yi'ta."

"Right then, Yi'ta. I happen to live in the apartment below, and I heard a noise that struck me as quite curious, the opening of some sort of gate, perhaps. And thusly, I ventured to discover its source."

Yi'ta grins, revealing a mouth full of yellow-white canine teeth that burst forth from black gums. "Ah, yes. Curiosity… humans are quite curious, I have read. We have a saying, 'curiosity killed the human.'"

"Cat." Another goblin, with patchwork overalls and an uncovered head of short, tufty hair, peeks from around the bell she cling to and corrects Yi'ta. "Curiosity killed the cat. Hubris killed the human."

"Right, right."

You intercede: "I admit I'm near dying to know what you're constructing up here."

"Of course," Yi'ta answers, staring at his clipboard and making some notes. "What we have here is a sonalopticloopticamplificator. Nothing special, really, in its construction, but its purpose," Yi'ta looks up and catches your eye with his own, "its purpose is to free our people."

The workgoblin from the bell saunters over and whispers into Yi'ta's ear. Yi'ta nods, and the workgoblin looks at you once more.

"We could use your help," Yi'ta says.

"I'm afraid I've never been much for mechanical construction," you admit.

"There are other ways you could help us."

"Very well then," you say, because you certainly had nothing more interesting to do. "How may I be of service?"

"Three ways, really. You see, we goblins are preparing for revolution. We've tried every peaceful method in our power to be free of the gnomes, but to no avail. We could use your help up here: as a human, you would be the perfect messenger for contacting our fellows in the other city towers. Or you could venture below, to the gnomish city of Hak'kal, and beseech them for liberty on our behalf. Finally, if you'd like, we could use another pair of arms to swing a club when, all other options explored, the great goblin army ascends upon the gnomes."

"Descends," you say, attempting to correct the fellow.

"Pardon?"

"An army *descends* upon a foe, not *ascends*."

"No, no, the goblin camps are quite a bit below Hak'kal."

*To stay above and work as a messenger for the goblins, go to* **Sixteen** *(page 25).*

*To venture below as an ambassador to the gnomes, go to* **Twelve** *(page 17).*

*To forgo subtlety and volunteer to serve in the goblin's revolutionary army, go to* **Eighteen** *(page 29).*

### Ten

"Now see here," you say, holding your cane in a manner most unbefitting a gentleman, "I'll have none of this. You may not go about constructing any sort of device, machine, contraption, or gadget without written permission from the landlord."

"I'm sorry to hear you say that," says the goblin at your feet. "Hey Gu'dal," he shouts towards the rear of the room, "we've got breach of etiquette to concern ourselves with."

Every goblin pauses in their work for a single moment and stares over at you, some in disbelief, some in anger, others with what appears to be amusement. It suddenly occurs to you that, hallucinations or no, the critters outnumber you remarkably.

One lanky goblin works her way through the room, wearing a fine suit and tie, her ears hidden under a comically large and narrow top hat, a top hat so tall that it reaches nearly to your waist when it sits atop her head. But any hint of comedy is thrown aside quite soon as she draws a sword from her cane and approaches.

"Good sir, it is impolite to interrupt the work of gnomes, goblins, or kabouters. In our culture, this simply is not done. If you have objection to our activities, you should have filed it with us before the work began." Her voice is measured and polite, but the blade, while scarcely longer than a steak knife, seems quite threatening in her hands.

*To fight Gu'dal, and intimidate the other goblins into ceasing their destruction of the clock tower, turn to* **Fourteen** *(page 21).*

*To humbly apologize, go to* **Eleven** *(page 16).*

### Eleven

"Madam, I meant no offense at all. I'm afraid your customs are… unfamiliar to me," you say.

"It's not me you need to apologize too. It's Yi'ta here, and everyone else, really. You're going to have to apologize to them."

"All of them?"

"All of them."

By twos and threes, each goblin takes leave of their measuring, hammering, tuning, and sawing to shake your hand and accept your apology. For each, you are required to explain the nature of your error, the depths of your sorrow, and the great degree to which you are humbled to be in their presence. With almost two-score of the little folk in the room, nearly a half-hour goes by.

"Now then," Yi'ta, the original goblin, says, "you have made your hubris known to us, and we will have no more of your intrusions. We will *not* be guiding you into our underworld, a world that may have delighted and intrigued you. Tonight you will *not* be embarking on an adventure that will change your life in a thousand ways. And if you speak of us, in the word either spoken or written, you will hang in this very tower by your entrails." Yi'ta smiles at you, a mouth full of tiny daggers.

You take your leave and return to your apartment. Tomorrow, you will begin to look for different housing. It does not pay to insult the goblinkin, it appears.

### The End

## Twelve

"Good, good," Yi'ta says. "Although I admit I'm a bit disappointed that we might not get to try out the sonalopti-cloopticamplificator. But we'll finish building it nonetheless, and if you fail at your task, we should have another opportunity in about six months. Six months might seem like a long time to you, of course, but we goblins are quite long-lived."

"Oh?" you ask, "what is a goblin's lifespan?"

"Why, the average goblin will live to be twenty-five, but we have on record goblins living up to the age of 37." Yi'ta clearly expects you to be impressed, and you decide to feign amazement rather than inform him of your own lifespan. And besides, the life expectancy for a poverty-stricken, depressive absinthe drunk like yourself is surely not much greater than that of a goblin.

"Anyhow, I think you might do well with company to show you the way to Hak'kal, yes? And I know just the goblin for the task. If there isn't to be a battle this morning we won't be needing her services anyhow." Yi'ta turns to face the workgoblins. "Gu'dal!"

A tall—well, tall for a goblin—and well-dressed goblin woman saunters up to you. She's got a thin, stretched look to her that extends up into her skinny top hat. She's twirling a cane and wearing a tailcoat. And when she speaks, she sounds like a talking bird. "Yi'ta?" she says when she approaches the two of you.

"If you could, I'd love for you to take…" Yi'ta looks back to you, "What is your name, sir? My manners must be in one of these pockets somewhere, because I obviously can't find them."

"Gregory," you say.

"Yes. I'd love for you to take Gregory here down below and show him to the gates to Hak'kal. He's going to speak on our behalf to the gnomes."

"No rebellion tonight?" Gu'dal asks.

"No, no. We're going to try again peacefully."

Gu'dal looks at you and grimaces. Previously, you had thought the *smile* of a goblin was disconcerting. "Alright, poltroon-pants. You don't mind that I call you poltroon-pants, do you?"

You look at her teeth and decide that yes, poltroon-pants is acceptable.

"Okay, I'll take you to the gates. Then you can do your talking. But if you think that talking to gnomes is safer than bashing them with wrenches, you're in for a bit of a surprise."

With no further words, Gu'dal turns and heads down the stairs.

A bit flustered, you follow. You take one last look at the door of your apartment, an apartment that has provided you such health and comfort.

Whatever object had lain upon the floorboards at the base of the steps is gone now, and as you reach the ground floor you realize that there is a goblin-sized doorway set into the side of the stairs. Through it, you see only blackness.

Gu'dal reaches her hand out to yours as she steps through the portal. You grasp it, and realize it is not as clammy as you thought it might be. She leads you down another flight of stairs in darkness.

After what feels like twenty minutes, you emerge from the side of a stone hallway that is lit by gas lamps set into sconces along the top. Fortunately, the ceiling is a good foot over your head. Steam pipes of various diameters and metals run the length of the hallway.

Your path slopes slightly in front of you, taking you deeper into the ground. As you walk along the corridor, you notice dozens of nooks and crannies brimming with strange machinery. Some of it—heating apparatus, water-pressure regulators, and ventilation fans—you recognize. But some of it is completely foreign to you: there are light-refracting crystals embedded into steam-engine bits; there are sets of tuning forks that linger on chords, some sonorous, some atonal. Most of it appears to be powered by the steam pipes that line the halls.

*To ask Gu'dal about the machinery, go to* **Twenty-Two** *(page 38).*

*To ask Gu'dal about the city you are approaching, go to* **Thirty-Two** *(page 51).*

*To continue forward unquestioningly, go to* **Thirty** *(page 49).*

### Thirteen

"Well I suppose I don't want to hang out with a bunch of pasty sods, now do I?" you say to A'gog. "What's say I come with you back to Haddlelint and we'll see what there is for a fellow like me to do."

A'gog grabs your hand and takes off at a bounding pace, forcing you to jog to keep up. "So, you any good with a gun?" he asks.

"Well, er, I can't say that I've too much experience in the matter," you respond, panting.

"What about strategy? You humans get into wars all the time, yeah?"

"Well, not so much myself personally, you understand," you demur. Demurring is particularly hard, by the way, since you are running at a decent clip and are forced to take several seconds between each word you utter.

"Whaddya get into then, up in your tower, if it isn't guns and strategizing?"

"Poems," you say, then stop running and lean against the wall of the tunnel. "I write poems. Would you like to hear one?"

"Oh god no," A'gog says.

You prepare to write him off as a philistine, but decide that as a member of another species, he's not too likely to have a sound enough understanding of human poetry to truly appreciate it. Better that a poem go unsaid than be spoken to unappreciative ears, you figure.

"We're almost there. C'mon." A'gog takes your hand again and leads you down a side tunnel, bounding once more and forcing you to run.

You enter a great natural cavern, larger than any room you'd thought could exist below the earth.

The entire space, vertically and horizontally, is laced with ropes and nets, some woven into nests like beehives, others forming intricate and beautiful patterns set against the backdrop of wondrous cave formations. And the air, the ground, even the ceiling of the place is bustling with goblins who crawl and swing and run, who dart to and fro carrying loads several times larger than themselves, who disappear down side tunnels bearing picks or who return, exhausted. Some cook, others play games on the floor, others look drunk. They tinker with devices well beyond your limited experience, and they play instruments that might be mistaken for work machines.

"Haddlelint, eh?" you say, taken aback, amazed, and quite a bit excited.

"Biggest town we got left. Kinda small, of course, but it's home." A'gog ambles to a faucet set into the stone wall and washes his hands. "I'm going to go get dinner. Might want to introduce yourself to your fans."

You turn from the old green man and realize that you're surrounded by other goblins. But it's not adoration you see in their eyes: it's curiosity and malice. Well, maybe not malice, but it's really hard to be certain when people have pointy yellow teeth and carry pickaxes.

"*Qui est tu?*" one of the more pugilistic of the little people demands.

"Look, I don't speak French. It's dreadfully embarrassing, I know. But I've only been here less than a year–"

"Who are you?" the goblin repeats, this time in passable English.

"Oh, that. The name's Gregory. And you?" You stick out your hand, which is ignored by the goblin.

"We're preparing for war. In less than six hours, we're going to storm the gates of Hak'kal, the gnomish capital, and lay waste to the city. The gnomes have enslaved us, but we will have both freedom and vengeance. Are you going to help us?"

*To insist that violence and retribution are not the most appropriate responses to the situation, go to* **Twenty-Six** *(page 43).*

*To toss your hat in with the goblins and prepare to join them in their battle, go to* **Twenty-One** *(page 35).*

## Fourteen

Your cane already raised, you attempt to land a crashing blow upon the skull of the sword-wielding woman, one that might seem heroic were it landed upon a person of your own stature. One that might have at least seemed worthwhile if it had connected at all.

Deft as housefly, Gu'dal skips to the side of your blow and cuts your hamstring. You collapse, and before you have time to breathe, your lungs are punctured, your cane-hand is cut, and your eyes are destroyed.

It takes longer than you thought it might to die, suffocating in your own blood.

## The End

### Fifteen

"Well I really think it's best to confront problems quite directly. And I suspect that I'm quite a bit larger than one of these gnomish chaps, aren't I? I'd really like to talk to one of them in person, and I suspect I can talk some sense into it."

"Are you that good with words?" A'gog asks.

"Well, no, not really." You take off your bowler and scratch your scalp. "But I suppose I've not much sense, either, so I thought I might as well try."

"I would have preferred you to serve some purpose, but, well, I believe in nothing if not autonomy. Take this tunnel," A'gog points to your right, "and take your first six lefts, then your fourth right, then the next left. You'll walk right into the front gates. Can't miss them."

A'gog turns and begins to walk opposite the way that you've been directed.

You shrug, a meaningless gesture since no one is around to see it, then follow A'gog's directions. An hour's walk—and no small amount of second-guessing your decision to confront the gnomes—later, you find yourself in an open, natural cavern. You're dwarfed by two gigantic, inlaid metal doors and are greeted by two creatures that look like nothing so much as half-size deep-sea divers.

Each of the guards bears a bizarre rifle with slowly spinning crystals along its barrel and wears a brass-and-glass helmet that disguises their face. The gnomes are twice as tall as A'gog was— meaning they might reach your shoulder with their hands outstretched—and they're both, well, fearsome.

There's something frightening about things that are completely alien to your experience, particularly when those things are pointing ornate and indecipherable weapons at your head and chest.

"Good morrow to you," you say, remembering your manners.

"*Va te faire foutre*," one of the guards says. You don't remember the translation of that particular phrase remarkably well, but you're reasonably certain that it isn't a term of endearment.

"Wait. Sit. No movement," the other guard says, in heavily accented English.

You decide that decorum require that you follow these instructions, so you sit. The ruder gnome walks over to a voice-horn set into the doorway and speaks into it. Moments later, the gates open and you catch a glimpse of a marvelous underground metropolis filled to overflowing with colored light and fantastical clockwork.

A gnome marches out the door, this one wearing a helmet that reveals his face to be rather like that of an angry, pre-pubescent boy. On top of his helmet is a quarter-life-sized statue of himself. He wears a uniform that seems to be a mockery of an aboveground military commander's, replete with medals, badges, and pins of all sorts—including at least one that you recognize as a campaign pin for a political candidate in aboveground France. You open your mouth to laugh at him—consider yourself rude if you will, but the fellow is quite humorous looking—but then shut it when you remember that you're in a cavern miles from your home and are surrounded by armed guards.

"This will be very simple for you. You are to be our guest, for as long or short of a time as you would like." The officer walks up to where you sit as he speaks, and he sounds gruff but not unfriendly. "But first, a test. A personality test."

From under his coat jacket, the officer pulls out a glass bottle of dark liquid. One of the guards rushes forward and offers a snifter, and the officer pours three fingers of what smells quite a bit like brandy into it.

"I will leave you with this, then go confer with my superiors. If, when I return, you have not drunk a sip of this brandy, you may join us as our guest in Hak'kal for as long as you would like, and all of your drinking and smoking will be utterly without cost. But if you prefer, you may drink this glass now, and although you may stay for some time in our city, no one will be permitted to serve you alcohol."

The officer walks away, and you think about his offer. Perhaps these gnomes have a greater sense of social responsibility than the goblin had led you to believe. After all, a man who cannot abstain from drinking for a half an hour would most likely abuse a bottomless glass. But one who can hold themself back perhaps could be trusted with such a responsibility. It's a curious situation, you decide.

*To drink the brandy because, well, it's there, go to* **Twenty-Five** *(page 42).*

*To abstain in the hopes of procuring more alcohol—and did he mention something about smoking?—then go to* **Twenty-Eight** *(page 46).*

### Sixteen

"Excellent," Yi'ta says when you tell him your decision. "We've work to set you to this very moment."

"Not in the morning?" you ask.

"Indeed not. No time for such things as sleep. No extra time whatsoever. In fact, our task will be accomplished at precisely seven-fifteen abovetime or it won't be accomplished at all."

"Why's that?" you ask.

Yi'ta pulls an elaborate sextant from a sheath at his belt. "It has to do with the longitude we're at, of course, and the alignment of the sun. In order for the astral soundwaves to detonate in the correct location, considering our position and the two other contextual placements of sonaloptic–

"Well, suffice it to say there will not be time for sleeping. I need you to go to the secondary tower with this report," he hands you a thin, hardbound journal, "and follow any instructions that they might have for you there. I needn't tell you that this report *must not* fall into the wrong hands. If you succeed, you will be a hero to all the underfolk. Well, except to the gnomes of course."

You open the report and look inside. The writing—if indeed it *is* writing at all—looks a bit like Arabic, if Arabic were entirely straight lines at right angles to one another.

"How do I–" you begin to ask.

"Gu'dal will show you the way." Yi'ta turns to the back of the belfry and shouts. "Gu'dal!"

A lanky goblin woman in a fancy tailcoat and black tie saunters over, her ears hidden within a tall, thin top hat, one that extends half again her height above her. She affects the use of a cane—something you are quite understanding of. When she is near, she smiles in the menacing way you now attribute to all of goblinkind.

"We have little time to waste, I fear," Gu'dal says. Her voice and accent, like Yi'ta's, remind you of the speaking raven you once saw at a circus performer's opium den.

Gu'dal, whose eyes reach your knees and whose hat reaches your thigh, grabs your pale hand in her green one and leads you down the stairs and onto the lamplit streets beyond.

*To ask Gu'dal about the task at hand, go to* **Nineteen** *(page 32).*

*To ask Gu'dal about herself, go to* **Twenty-Three** *(page 39).*

*To continue on in silence, go to* **Thirty-One** *(page 49).*

## Seventeen

"They eat well, in the suburbs?" you ask.

"Better 'n a goblin, that's certain," A'gog replies.

"Right then, it's settled. To Underburg. I know a thing or two about getting a rise out of folks who think they're all proper and happy."

"Do you always think with your stomach?" There seems to be genuine appreciation in A'gog's voice.

"Oh no," you say. "Before I've had anything to drink, I think with my... whatever the organ is that makes you want booze."

"Brain."

"Right then, before I'm drunk, I think with my brain."

A'gog giggles and bounces up and down in the tunnel, his long green ears a'flapping. And it occurs to you that you haven't been thinking with your stomach *or* your brain. It takes you a moment, but you decide you've been thinking with your heart. But that sounds terribly cliché, and certainly won't make it into your poetry come the morning. Instead, you decide, you have been thinking with your wormwood.

A'gog takes your hand and breaks into a sprint, moving significantly faster than you would expect a green little monster who can barely meet eyes with your kneecaps to go, and you are forced into a swift jog to keep pace.

You fly down tunnels for twenty minutes and stop in front of a vent that A'gog immediately begins to disassemble.

"So what's your plan? Give a good rousing speech? You Brits are good for speeches, is what I hear. I can interpret, too."

"No," you say. "Speeches are good for riling up people with nothing to lose, people who maybe were thinking about giving it a go but just never really made up their minds."

"What then?"

"We're going to destroy their way of life," you say. In the dimly-lit hallway, you don't know if A'gog can see your manic grin. You've never had much love for the middle class. At least the upper class knows how to party. The middle class? Worse than useless.

"Huh," A'gog says. The vent comes off the wall, revealing a crawlspace. Well, a walk-space for A'gog. A crawlspace for you. "How you going to do that?"

"I don't know yet. What's the situation like in Underburg?"

You get on hands and knees and crawl into the wind. It's quite painstaking and—after the first bend in the tunnel—dark. A'gog leads the way, and you follow his voice while he apprises you.

"It's pitch black, it is. Like I was saying before, the kabouters don't see with their eyes, they see with their ears. They screech—it's a bit unnerving, just to warn you—and know where everything is."

"Blind as a bat?" you suggest.

"Bats can see with their eyes. No, they're blind as a cave critter. Only without the weird feeler-thingies. But kinda ugly like one, too. Anyhow, Underburg… the gnomes don't bother to guard Underburg. The stupid kabouters have been slaves so long they don't know they're slaves."

"Yup, sounds like the middle class to me. What are their houses made of?"

"Snot. They excrete a kind of sticky paste through their noses. It's good glue, but if you have enough time and enough kabouters, you can build yourself a hive."

"Huh. Is it flammable?"

"Sure."

"You've a lighter?" you ask.

"Of course. Why, you've some opium?"

"No, no. I just think I have a plan."

"Good, we're nearly there."

*To set about incinerating the town of Underburg in the hopes that the chaos that ensues will spark the revolutionary potential and desire of the kabouters, go to* **Twenty-Nine** *(page 47).*

*To get into the city first and develop some sort of stunning— and only metaphorically incendiary—plan, go to* **Twenty-Four** *(page 41).*

## Eighteen

"I never been one to speak amiably with tyrants, nor one to costume my emotions. I'm also *dreadfully* afraid of missing anything interesting. So I suppose I shall volunteer myself, an infantryman in the ranks of goblins?"

Yi'ta looks you up and down, no doubt gauging your suitability for the task you've chosen to undertake. "Are you drunk?" he asks.

"Most likely," you say.

"Are you this brave when you're sober?" he asks.

"I'm afraid not."

"Well then, please ascertain you have enough alcohol to keep yourself intoxicated until after our glorious victory, yes?"

"I wouldn't dream of venturing out without ample spirits," you say. Inside your head, you're beginning to laugh. What an excellent adventure this shall be!

A tall—well, tall for a goblin—goblin woman approaches you, grinning quite mischievously. Although, you realize, it's possible that she could be grinning without the slightest trace of mischief. That's the thing about anthropomorphizing other creatures—it doesn't work.

"Gu'dal," the new goblin says, thrusting her hand out at you.

"Gregory," you say, and shake. Your hand quite engulfs hers, and she digs her nails into your palm, perhaps by accident.

Gu'dal is wearing a patchwork tailcoat over tight leather pants that show her legs to be as thin as lines. She bears a cane, its head carved into the likeness of some sort of swine-faced demon, and wears a comical stovetop hat that makes her some-how seem even thinner.

"You'll come down below with us then, storm the gates as part of the greatest horde these caverns have ever seen?"

"Er… yes." You avoid letting yourself reconsider. You meant it when you said that you weep for lost opportunity. How could you *not* volunteer to fight in an army of goblins? Besides, odds are good that you're merely hallucinating. It wouldn't be the first time.

Gu'dal leads you out of the belfry and down the stairs. Whatever that bundle at the base of the tower had been, it is gone now. But there *is* a goblin-sized archway mysteriously set into the base of the stairs. Your guide takes your hand in hers—this time without clawing you—and you crouch to follow her through the door and into the darkness.

Fortunately, after a few steps, you've room enough to walk upright down the stairs. And, what's more, your eyes begin to adjust to the dark. Up ahead, you see the faint glow of gaslight.

At the base of the steps, you find yourself in what looks to be a service tunnel, pipes of all diameters running along the ceiling and walls. Every few dozen yards is a dim gaslight, and spaced further apart than that are vents that spill fresh—well fresh*er*—air into the tunnel.

You're led along this tunnel at a remarkable speed—despite her short legs, Gu'dal walks as fast as yourself—and find yourself heading deeper and deeper underground.

You come into a great chamber, the breadth and height of an opera house. There are nets strung chaotically throughout the chamber, balconies and hammocks set randomly throughout. And sitting, standing, hanging, clambering, and snoring within are hundreds—dare you guess thousands?—of goblins, all dressed in makeshift spiky armor, all wielding a fantastical array of edged, blunt, and projectile weapons. And nearly all of them look like they are having a great deal of fun.

"You're preparing for war?" you ask Gu'dal.

"Of course," she replies.

"I had expected something more, *somber*, I suppose."

Gu'dal doesn't answer you.

Right by the entrance, you see three gray-haired goblins sitting on their helmets, shuffling clay tiles about in front of them. It's quite clear that they are playing a drinking game.

You decide that you like the goblins.

"Well, if all goes as we hope, we should be underway within the next few hours. Do you want to be right up in front, make sure you catch all the action?" Gu'dal looks enchanted, enthralled, at the prospect of going to war against the gnomes.

*To join the front of the horde, go to* **Twenty** *(page 34).*

*To demure and find yourself a place near the back, go to* **Twenty-Seven** *(page 45).*

## Nineteen

"What is that we're carrying, anyhow?" you ask.

"I don't understand all of it," Gu'dal says. "But basically, we're building amplifiers and receivers in the belltowers. We'll toll them in certain sequences—those sequences are recorded in the notebook—and if everything is lined up correctly, blam-o."

"Blam-o?"

"We strike down the gates to Hak'kal and flow through like stormwater, washing their sins away with blood." Gu'dal gets a bit of spring in her step as she describes the glorious revolution, flashing her fangs, and you can't help but wonder if you're on the right side.

"But what is Hak'kal?"

"Hak'kal is a monster. We goblins used to have a holy cave filled with food and riches. It was never depleted, because we were careful; we didn't live in the cave, we just went there to gather. Then the gnomes came and built a city in our holy cave. Within ten years they'd exhausted their resources and now we goblins are forced to mine their metals. The slaves they brought with them, the kabouters, they gather all their food. The gnomes live like happy little kings and we goblins are their slaves. Until tomorrow. Then we'll—

"Watch out!" Gu'dal says, pulling you into an alley.

"What?" you whisper, your back against the darkened brick, but Gu'dal puts her hand over her mouth, signaling you into silence.

As you watch from the darkness, three police officers stroll by on their rounds, swinging truncheons at their sides. You're about to step out of the alley—skulking usually drawing more attention than simply walking—when you see what appears to be a child scurry after them.

"That's a gnome," Gu'dal whispers in your ear. You turn around and see that your friend is suddenly at your eye level: Gu'dal is clinging to the brick with claws on her hands and feet.

You stare after the retreating gnome. If it weren't for the friendly green monster hiding in the alley next to you, you would never believe that the child-like silhouette was anything other than just that—a child.

The gendarmes past, you slip out of the alley and continue another three blocks to the secondary tower.

*Go to* **Thirty-Three** *(page 52).*

## Twenty

"Of course! I'd hate to miss any of the fun," you say. You're not sure why you say it. But say it you do.

Gu'dal smiles at you, quite charming in her skeletal, green, pointy-toothed-and-black-gummed kind of way. It seems like everyone you know on the surface has a carefully practiced dispassion, a lack of interest in anything that matters to the real world. (Excepting your brother, of course, who was exiled for sedition.) But down here, people seem to care about something.

You make your way up to the front of the room, carefully stepping over sleeping goblins, narrowly avoiding being caught in the middle of a lively game of "catch the axe-head."

When you reach the front of the crowd, up near a large set of steel doors that you presume to lead towards Hak'kal, you find a cut-off stalagmite to sit upon and, before you know it, fall asleep.

Ten seconds or three hours later, you're roused by a booming, high-pitched voice. Dangling by a rope from the ceiling, a large goblin woman hangs in plate armor that looks cobbled from cookware. You realize that she's giving a speech.

Gu'dal translates parts of it for you: "'Goblins of the mines, goblins of the fields. Our parents' parents' parents' parents' parents' parents'—sorry, there's a simpler word for it in Goblin—'lived here in these tunnels. They lived honestly. They worked when it pleased them, invented only what was worth inventing. They built and ventilated these tunnels. They ate the mushrooms right off the walls! They sang and they danced. Sometimes they fought one another, sure. Sometimes they stole children from the humans above. But it is *not* as the gnomes will say, is it?'"

The entire crowd roared, "*Hin!*" You presume this to be the word for "no."

"'Every generation, we have tried to cast off our chains. Every generation, we have tried to destroy Hak'kal, only to fail! Will it be any different this time?"

As one voice, the crowd screams "*Hin!*" You begin to doubt your ability to guess what words mean.

"'We will fight and we will die! We will fight and we will die!'" Gu'dal whispers this last bit of translation to you, then joins in the chant. "*Gad urrthrane gad urrthrus! Gad urrthrane gad urrthrus!*"

You pull a flask of brandy from its place in your vest pocket and drain it in one, long pull. Unfortunately, you're still not feeling precisely "in the moment," so you take your hipflask from its place tucked into your belt and begin to sip the grain alcohol within. Eventually, your mind goes where you want it to go. "*Gad urrhtrane gad urrthrus! Gad urrthrane gad urrthrus!*" you chant. And suicidal a chant it might be, it gets to you. You're ready. Ready to fight, ready to die.

*Go to* **Thirty-Nine** *(page 65).*

### Twenty-One

"These gnomish chaps," you ask, "are they as short as you all?"

"Oh no," the goblin says, "each one is twice as tall as a goblin and weighs easily up to four stone!"

"I'll be happy to help," you say, because you weigh ten stone and if there's a fight you can win, it's one against a foe half your height and stature.

"Hurrah!" a goblin—a different one—lets out. And suddenly a dozen small hands are upon you, dragging you along to join the rest of the horde. As one, you march out of the town, through a long tunnel, and into a tall room that looks almost like an opera hall: a tall cylinder with a floor that is sloped down towards… well, instead of a stage there is a massive set of steel doors.

And instead of an audience, there are hundreds, maybe even thousands, of goblins dressed for war. But if you'd hoped for a somber war party, you have come to the wrong cavern. Well, you are rarely hoping for a somber party of any sort, so you're most likely quite delighted: the goblins prance and play and drink—and copulate, it seems, if those two suspended in a net fifteen feet above your head are doing what you think they are doing—all while dressed in a crazy assortment of mismatched armor and wielding any number of misappropriated tools.

A'gog steps up and finds you, leads you to the front of the crowd. "Wouldn't want to miss anything, I wouldn't, and my eyesight isn't what it once was."

Looking at the crowd around you, you suddenly feel quite underdressed. Certainly, you'd look impeccable—well, a bit dusty—at a soirée, but you haven't a stitch of armor about you, and while your cane is quite handy for threatening the children of beggars, you wouldn't expect it to handle a full-fledged war.

It's when you remember the existence of guns that your blood turns to ice. You're four times as tall as any other target.

"Tell me," you ask A'gog, "do the gnomes have guns?"

"No, no, of course not. A gun would be too dangerous underground. What if they struck a pipe? The pressure would blow the whole tunnel, it would."

Somehow, this relieves you a little bit. But your guide continues:

"No, they don't use guns. They use lightrifles."

You decide you don't want to know what a lightrifle is. Ignorance may not be bliss, but you don't see any good place to relieve yourself and therefore "frightful sounding" sounds better than "the certainty of doom" that you're afraid you might come to understand.

Your fretting is interrupted by the dramatic descent from the ceiling—via rope—of a rather large goblin woman wearing armor that is clearly piecemeal assembled from cookware. She speaks in a loud, clear, high-pitched voice, and stirs great emotion in the room. It's a shame you can't understand what she's saying.

"What's she saying," you ask A'gog. Nearby, someone shushes you.

"Eh, you know. The same old crap. We goblins are great, the gnomes killed everything good. We have to fight. We won't win… you know, a battle speech."

"We won't win?" you ask, because you feel quite invested in a victorious outcome for the side that you have chosen nearly at random.

You are shushed again, and A'gog doesn't translate anything more.

The crowd gets driven to a fervor, many of them weeping red tears, many of them screaming, chanting, banging their weapons against their armor. Then…

Then the chanting stops, and the great doors in front of you stay closed. Someone makes an announcement.

A'gog then addresses the room. In English, probably for your sake. "I don't care. So Yi'ta messed up. Yi'ta always messes up. I don't know about any of you, but I'm going to fight, because I'm an old man and I probably won't even be around next chance we get. If I'm gonna die, I want to die drunk at the hands of our foes! And I'm going to bring this poor, moronic Englishman with me!"

You pull a small flask from your hatband and empty it.

Everyone starts to shuffle out of the room, back towards the goblin town. The battle is over, it seems, before it has begun. Even the woman with her battle-speech departs, leaving you alone in the chamber with A'gog.

"Well, how about it?" he asks.

*To demur and ask for directions back to your tower, go to* **Thirty-Seven** *(page 60).*

*To pass a flask of brandy and see what you can do about nearly single-handedly laying siege to a city full of strange inventors, go to* **Thirty-Five** *(page 56).*

## Twenty-Two

"We make it, you know," Gu'dal says, stopping to run her fingers along a set of small whistles set into one pipe. "The gnomes design it, but it's not like we couldn't do that ourselves. This one sounds an alarm if the pressure has built up too high. It has notes for the gnomes, and higher pitched tones that only us goblins can hear."

Your guide takes her hands off of the pipes and turns to look at you. "The gnomes will tell you, when you talk to them, that they've civilized us. That we do this work and that we are appreciative of it. That *they* taught *us* the wonders of technology. It's not true. One hundred and seventy years ago, when Hak'kal was built, we goblins already knew about light and sound. All they brought was steam. Steam, and, of course, slavery."

You walk awhile longer while you consider what she said. It's a strange, dark place, this underground. You begin to hope, for what will not be the last time, that you're indeed hallucinating this whole experience.

"We're here," Gu'dal says. "The gates to Hak'kal are just around the corner."

*Go to* **Forty** *(page 68).*


## Twenty-Three

"Tell me a bit about yourself," you say to Gu'dal.

"What?" She looks genuinely concerned. "Why?"

"I'm curious, you know. I've never met a goblin before."

"Well I've never met a human either, but I'm not going to go sticking my ears into your business."

"You've never met a human? Really?" You walk down the deserted cobblestone street, a bit of fog rising from sewer grates.

"No, of course not. In the resistance, it's just diplomats who work aboveground. This is the first time any of those engineers or us warriors have ever seen the sky, tell you the truth."

You look up into the dark heavens above you, catching what stars you can past the streetlamp's glow. You think about what it would be like to have never had an expanse above you, and you shudder. "You're a warrior, then?" you ask, looking up at Orion.

"Been studying since my head reached only to your shins. In between work shifts, we drill. It's the best thing in life, training. We don't make it look like training, of course. The gnomes think we're just dancing."

"How could someone mistake militia training for dancing?"

"Never underestimate the civilized's contempt for the tribal. We sing, do things in rhythm, and they think it's art. In fact, I'll tell you a story. My uncle, see, he was a bomb maker. He did demolitions for mining, mostly, of course, but he studied how to take down the doors to Hak'kal. He even built a machine for it, the craziest contraption you'll ever see, with pneumatics and a drilling arm and optical systems to correctly orient itself. Thing was, three days before he was going to put into place, only hours before he was going to fill it up with gunpowder, the gnomes did a sweep through our camp. They saw his machine and they asked him what it was. 'Art', he said, and the damn thing is in a museum in Hak'kal. I saw once when I was–

"Watch out!" Gu'dal yells, dragging you into a nearby alley.

"What?" you whisper. But Gu'dal puts her hand over her mouth. Three police officers walk past, swinging truncheons, one whistling a lively folk tune. You press your back further to the wall, not wanting to be seen skulking about in alleys, and you see what looks like a child hurrying along behind them.

"That's a gnome," Gu'dal whispers from her newfound perch atop a trash can.

"How do you know?" you whisper back.

Just then the child-or-gnome barks an order at the gendarmes, one that you don't understand, and the police obey, turning into the alley across the street from you. No child would be ordering the police about, of course. And with a friendly green monster standing beside you in the shadows, you're willing to believe a lot more than usual.

Gu'dal grabs your hand and you find your way through the alley as quickly and silently as you can. You make it to the next street and reach the first tower on your rounds.

*Go to* **Thirty-Three** *(page 52).*

## Twenty-Four

A'gog passes you his lighter and you strike it, witnessing a bizarre scene. A hatch in the floor opens onto a rope ladder and darkness. A green little man—A'gog—stands poised to descend, and right behind him stands perhaps the strangest looking creature you've ever seen. He's taller than the goblin and shorter than you, but it's hard to discern his height in the dim light and the strange cramped corridor. His skin is paler than that of a sickly white fellow; his eyes are enormous unseeing orbs. His ears are deranged, maybe like an elephant's. And he's hyperventilating, you think. Only, you know, silently.

"Hello?" you ask.

"Good morrow. Are you here with the Aboveground?" The stranger speaks with excellent English, although you detect a hint of a Russian accent.

"Yes," you say, thinking that he means the surface of the earth.

"Hell no," A'gog corrects.

"What?" the kabouter—what else could he be?—asks.

"We're not with those wimpy city gnomes."

"Oh," you say. "Is that like, how, up above, we have, you know, the Underground?"

"Is that the resistance movement that is largely incompetent and people mostly just join so that they can be impressed with themselves and have sex?"

"Well," you think. "I've never heard it put that way before, but... yes."

"Then yes. The Aboveground is like your Underground. Only the Underground is aboveground, and the Aboveground is underground, of course."

"Of course," you say. This calls for a drink, and the flask in your boot happily obliges. You pass it to your two companions, who both drink deeply.

"So you're not with the Aboveground. Are you working with the gnomes?"

"I'll have your ears, you snotty bastard!" A'gog reaches to grab the stranger.

You try to hold him back, but no sooner is your hand on his shoulder than you get kicked something vicious in the chest.

"Sorry, sorry," the kabouter says. "I offer you a sincere apology, my good goblin. Believe me, I would not have thought you to be a—"

"You'd better not have," A'gog grumps.

"Look, I'm quite confused," you say, "so I'll just lay it all out. My handsome, forgiving, and very-much-not-a-traitor friend A'gog and I were on our way to Underburg to see what kind of trouble we could stir up, see if we couldn't recruit some of you capable folks for a full-scale revolution."

"And how did you think to do that?"

*To suggest minor shenanigans that are likely to draw the ire of the gnomish guards, and therefore spark anti-colonial sentiment within the kabouters, go to* **Thirty-Eight** *(page 62).*

*To propose that you gather up all who will listen and persuade them with your charisma and oratory prowess, go to* **Thirty-Six** *(page 58).*

## Twenty-Five

The brandy is incredibly strong, incredibly tasty. It also appears to be drugged.

When you wake, you're in an opium den, surrounded by fellow humans. Between the haze of drugs and the endless decanters of brandy, though, you never do make sense of your situation.

Perhaps this is the peak of your life: you've found the bar that there is no need to stumble home from, the opium den never raided by police. You rouse and slumber at random intervals, and never again learn to distinguish dream-state from reality.

In a rare moment of lucidity, you decide that you don't care.

Eventually, the drugs seep so deeply into your brain that you fail to notice the distinction between living and death. You die, most likely, perhaps years or decades or hours after arriving in Hak'kal, in a city-sponsored prison for those prone to excess. You don't remember exactly how to distinguish pleasure from sorrow, but you have the distinct impression that you die quite happy.

**The End**

## Twenty-Six

"Oh heavens no," you say. "I don't see myself as much of a combatant, not really."

"Coward, are you?" asks the one who menaces you currently.

"Why, no!" you say, then think of a bigger lie to disguise that smaller one. "It's just that, well, I don't believe in it. I don't believe in war."

"Well I don't believe in *grash'nar*," the goblin says, the word foreign and guttural and honestly quite frightening, "but that didn't keep one from eating my older brother!"

The rest of the goblins laugh at this macabre humor, but it merely emboldens your stance.

"Now see here, you can't just go around enacting vengeance all of the time. It's no way to solve the problem of violence. You can't solve anger with a sword any more than you can cure sobriety with abstinence!"

"Your brain is made out of those little flecked mushrooms, the ones that look like the penis of a rat." With this bizarre insult, the angry goblin walks away. The rest of the crowd soon follows suit, and you're left standing quite confused in the midst of a great deal of hubbub. Most of the town's goblins appear to be assembling a good bit distant from you, many of them wearing makeshift armor and wielding nasty looking engineering and mining tools.

Two goblins approach you, holding hands and dressed quite unlike the rest of their fellows. Where most of the goblins in your sight are wearing rag-tag suits, engineering clothes, or battle raiment, these wear thick woolen tunics embroidered with the symbols of the arcane that you recognize from the alchemist phase that you went through in your youth.

"We heard your words, friend, and believe you," the shorter of the two goblins says.

"You do? Why?" you ask, unable to catch yourself.

"Because we have uttered them ourselves, though we too were met with scorn. What our brethren fail to understand is that the problems we goblins face are internal. We must defeat the colonization of our brains, the colonization of prejudice and resentment, before we can begin to understand the problem outside of us. Don't you agree?"

"Sure," you say, a bit uncertain as to what you are agreeing with.

"You must join us!" says the second goblin, the taller one. "We have battles to fight, yes, but they are battles of perception and understanding, not retribution. Our weapons are our vapors, our armor is our mind."

"Yeah, join us." says the first goblin, and flashes you an all-fanged smile.

*To turn down the offer, go to* **Thirty-Four** *(page 53).*

*To join the strange, peaceful goblins, go to* **Forty-One** *(page 71).*

### Twenty-Seven

"Well, you see," you begin, your mind searching around for a suitable excuse. "I'm quite tall, you understand. An easy target. But also, quite useful tactically. I can survey the situation more effectively if I'm at a more appreciable distance…"

While you're talking, Gu'dal looks at you with a face that may or may not be condemnation, then walks to the front of the room, leaving you behind.

"Yes, well…" you begin, talking to yourself.

"Makes sense to me," a young-looking goblin man says, from his position hanging in a net very close to right above your head.

"It does?" you ask.

"Certainly. And why, I bet you'd make a first-class goblin-thrower, too, when the front lines thin out and we need reinforcements."

"Of course," you say. "Naturally."

You find a spot to lean against the wall near the back of the room, and soon fall asleep.

Just as you being to have a pleasant dream about a seductive haberdasher, you're woken by someone giving a speech. High above the crowd, dangling from a rope, a powerful-looking goblin woman armored with cast-iron pots and pans addresses the room in a shrill but charismatic voice.

Unfortunately, you've no clue what she's saying. The crowd responds a few times, gathering energy, then begins to chant. It sounds like "God earth rain, god earth rush" to you, so that's what you chant, in between sips of whisky from the flask in your boot.

"God earth rain, god earth rush! God earth rain, god earth rush!"

It gets your blood going, even if it's gibberish. You're ready to fight.

Gu'dal emerges from the front of the room and looks at you appraisingly, but you keep chanting. The alcohol and the power of the crowd have gotten to you. Gu'dal smiles her disconcerting smile.

*Go to* **Thirty-Nine** *(page 65).*

## Twenty-Eight

Your willpower overcomes your oft-drunken mind and you hold the glass in your hands for a half-hour before the captain returns. Upon seeing the brandy remaining in the snifter, a look of alarm crosses his face and he blows a whistle.

Seven heavily-armed riflegnomes double-step march through the gates and arrest you bodily, bludgeoning you into unconsciousness.

When you awaken, you find yourself high above the city, perched naked in a human-sized birdcage hanging by a chain from a stalactite. On the floor of the cage is a small bowl filled with something that smells like oatmeal. Next to it is a sign, written in sixteen different languages. In English, it says: "Sing, and you eat. The louder and more beautifully you sing, the better you eat."

Across the ceiling of the vast cavern you see other birdcages, filled with naked humans of all ages. The cage closest to you holds a man even younger than yourself, one who seems to be signaling to you by holding his arms out at angles.

It takes you hours to decipher the semaphore code he's using, but eventually you learn enough to communicate.

"Don't speak aloud, or they'll hurt us," he says.

"Alright," you respond, laboring over each letter of the code.

"You refrained from drinking the brandy, didn't you? Bad idea. Means you're smart enough that you might have caused trouble."

Shortly after this communication, the man in the cage near you is taken roughly away by gnomes on an impossibly tall ladder. He never returns.

When it comes your turn to sing, you sing. For years and years, you sing. Until the end of your life, you sing in your birdcage above the city.

**The End**

## Twenty-Nine

A'gog opens a hatch in the floor, though you can't see anything, and passes you his lighter.

You strike the flint, the wick catches, and you find yourself staring into the huge, unseeing eyes of a bizarre *thing*—not to be rude, but you certainly have a hard time finding another word to describe the creature. You jump with a start, smacking your head on the ceiling, and it takes off at a run down the crawlspace.

"Was that a, uh…"

"Kabouter? Yes. And he noticed us, as you might have guessed. Whatever it is we're going to do, we'd better do it quickly."

You look through the hatch, and see a metal-runged rope ladder dangling down into the darkness. You put your foot on the first rung, shrug, douse your flame, and descend.

Three hundred rungs—well, give or take a score, your fear of heights distracting your count for a good moment—later, you put your foot onto solid stone ground and re-strike your flame.

*Hive* was indeed an apt word. You're in the midst of a strange nightmare, shrunk down and thrust into the hive of a bee. Everything glistens and looks oozy. There's no separation between buildings here; they all melt together. It's like you're in the belly of a terrible, terrible monster. And the monster smells *bad*.

You rush up to the nearest wall of snot and bring your flame to it. It takes only a moment before it catches, and A'gog screams, right behind you.

"I could kill you!" he says to you. "But I won't have to."

"What?"

The flames spread quickly, and you have to step back away from the heat. Soon the entire cavern seems to be burning. Including your rope ladder.

"Don't worry," you say, "the flames are dying as fast as they started."

"That's because they've used up all the oxygen," A'gog tells you.

"Exactly! See? Since we're in a cave, the fire can't last long enough to… oh."

And those are your last mortal words, because it turns out that you, like fire, require oxygen to breathe. You fall to the floor and suffocate, your skin scorched. An angry, angry old goblin dies beside you.

### The End

### Thirty

You walk down the hallway in a silence punctuated only by the echoes of your footsteps and by Gu'dal's loud breathing. Eventually, Gu'dal stops.

"The gates to Hak'kal are just around the corner," she says. "I'm not getting close. Good luck. And if you tell them about what we're doing up above, in your clock tower, I'll kill you in your sleep."

*Go to* **Forty** *(page 68).*

### Thirty-One

Gu'dal tells you where you're going and you set out, reasonably sure of your direction. You've only been in the city for about a year, but the two towers aren't far out of the area you know well.

The moon peeks through clouds above you, shining gibbous and pale. A few stars are out, calming you. What a horror it would be to live underground, you think, to spend your days without the heavens above.

Your mind wanders as the two of you walk in silence down the empty boulevards of your adopted home. You think about England, a land that is likely to be forever behind you, a land you honestly don't miss. And you think about your elder brother, whose footsteps you followed by moving to France. Then you think of him, deported to French Guinea, doomed to spend the rest of his life in the prison colony, and your mood turns sour. Perhaps there is something to this talk of revolution, you decide.

But your thoughts are soon interrupted.

"Police!" Gu'dal calls out, dragging you into the shadows of a nearby alley. As soon as you are off the street, she upturns a trash can and holds it up to you. "Put it on! Hurry!"

Before you have time to question to the sanity or hygienety of such an action, you obey. It's a tight fit, but you're able to sit on the ground, completely covered. Soon you hear several sets of boot steps approach. A high-pitched voice calls out in a language you don't understand and the police—as you assume them to be—begin to search the alley. You hold your breath as they come within inches of discovering you. And while you've committed no crime, being discovered under a trash can in an alley at this hour—with a goblin for a companion no less— would certainly be uncomfortable.

But the gendarmes don't find you, and a few minutes after their footsteps recede you uncover yourself and stand.

By some miracle, you smell no worse than you did when you started, and in no time at all you find yourself at the door to the first clock tower on your list.

*Go to* **Thirty-Three** *(page 52).*

## Thirty-Two

"Hak'kal?" The city's name is guttural, like the sound of some-one about to spit, or like something the Dutch would say. "It's the gnome's cultural center, to hear them tell of it. It's an impressive place; all kinds of towers spiring from the floor like stalagmites, and there's a huge university where no goblin may study. It's a city, a bit like the ones you've got up there. You've got to talk to 'em, you've got to tell them to let us goblins free. We can't work like this forever. Every generation is getting more and more used to slavery. It's just not right. Please." Gu'dal looks up at you, perhaps on the verge of tears.

"Alright," you say, "I'll do what I can. I'll try to talk the gnomes into letting you go." As soon as you say it aloud, you realize that you mean it. Sure, the goblins are strange and feisty and dangerous. But so are most of your friends. It won't do to have them stay enslaved.

"Well," Gu'dal says, "the gates to Hak'kal are just around the next corner. When I tell you good luck, I mean it. They're a deceitful bunch. I've no doubt they'll try to win you over to their side. We goblins have a saying, 'You can tell a goblin doesn't like you when they've stuck a knife in you. You can tell a gnome doesn't like you when they're offering you wine.'"

Gu'dal thinks for a moment, then continues. "Actually, that's kind of a racist saying. There are some good gnomes. It's just that good gnomes tend to wind up dead, at least in Hak'kal."

*Go to* **Forty** *(page 68).*

## Thirty-Three

The first clock tower on your list is squat and old, the stonework tarnished the color of smog, the clock face a mere ten meters above the cobbles. The door at the base is of iron-banded oak, and a padlock of thick steel holds it shut.

Before you've the chance to despair, Gu'dal removes a set of lock picks from a place of concealment in her hat and begins to work at the lock with the manual dexterity and finesse you've seen exhibited only by thieves, contraptors, and clowns. (Although most of those you've met in one of those categories might easily be lumped into the other two as well!)

While you keep watch in the pre-dawn fog, Gu'dal sets the wards into place, and the door opens before panic has a chance to overcome your slightly addled mind. You slip into the darkness beyond and find your way up the circular staircase until you reach the dimly-lit belfry.

The scene inside is similar to the one you have so recently left: workgoblins of all manner and of every shade of green are working at a ponderous speed to contrapt some device. But what stands out to you, aside from a certain solemnity, is the human gentleman of very advanced years who appears to be guiding them.

It is this man who approaches you—or rather, approaches Gu'dal. He hobbles over, making heavy use of his cane, and begins to converse with Gu'dal in a not-unpleasant tongue.

"Pardon me, sir," you interject, as the fellow looks remarkably English.

The man looks at you, his face contorted to mimic the look of a frightened dog that had been recently jabbed with the point of a cane.

Gu'dal, in turn, looks at you in obvious annoyance and pulls you aside for a moment's conference. "Mr. Babbage was a prisoner in Hak'kal for a decade before we effected his release. His taskmaster was an Englishman. I would leave the conversation to me."

Thusly chastised, you stand a bit away for the rest of the brief encounter. You see a wild animal buried under the gentleman's eyes, but Gu'dal manages her business and shortly you are out the door towards the next clock tower.

Half done, you are thinking, and not a bad bit of work. "The hero of goblinkind," they said, and you've never heard of a hero who pays for his or her own drinks.

But as your footsteps lighten at the prospect of goblin-financed hedonism, a patrol of policemen stop your path.

"*Arrêter-vous!*" they say.

You look up frightened, and what you presume to be a gnome steps out between the legs of two cops. "You've been tricked, human, and we've been tailing you. The goblin you escort is a wanted revolutionist, a terrorist. If she and her friends would have their way, this city and mine would fall into ruin and anarchy. Whatever she may have told you, she can't be trusted."

*To turn Gu'dal over to the gendarmes, go to* **Forty-Two** *(page 73).*

*To fight, go to* **Forty-Seven** *(page 78).*

*To try to appeal to the human police officers, go to* **Fifty-Three** *(page 85).*

## Thirty-Four

"No thank you," you say, "I think my place is here." You pointedly avoid mention of how obviously garish their clothes are or how clearly backwards they are for believing the gibberish you've been spouting.

The pair shrugs in unison and walk away.

"You fighting or not, British man?"

You turn around to find A'gog hopping up and down, his cane pressed into the cave floor, his long ears flapping so that he looks curiously like a green, talking rabbit tied to a stick. In fact, the image is so strange that you begin to giggle—quite rudely—at the sight.

A'gog bounces away, and the horde leaves the cavern. Somewhere, a great creak and moan of machinery shudders in the walls and you are left in total darkness, quite alone, not even a sound to keep you company.

You sit down on the warm stone floor, remove a flask from your vest pocket, and sip. Three long sips later, it's drained, and you lie down—quite logically, you feel—to sleep.

You do not even dream. And when you're roused by a pale, rude child wearing a diver's helmet and wielding a frighteningly complex rifle, you decide to take your lack of dreams as evidence that you are, indeed, dreaming this whole mad adventure. Thusly, you ignore the child.

Until he jabs you in the neck with the barrel of his gun.

"Bugger off," you say.

"Get up."

"I don't feel like it," you tell him, and pull your bowler down over your eyes, resuming a supine position.

"I will kill you, human."

"You're a human too," you say, growing ever more irritable. What's more, your head is pounding and your throat is quite dry.

"Get up!" The gnome bellows this in a voice deeper than any child's, deeper than any grown man's. It seems to shake the whole cavern, and for a moment you fear a cave-in. Then, when you realize you're almost never this hung over in dreams, you fear the rifle pointed into your throat.

"I'm sorry," you say, rising to a sitting position, "I had thought I was dreaming."

"You're not."

"I suppose you're a gnome, then?"

The child—correct that, gnome—in a diver's helmet nods.

"Well your whole war is foolishness. It's simply nonsensical."

"How is that?" the gnome asks, forcing you at gunpoint to stand and begin to leave the cavern.

More gnomes—in their absurd helmets—join you as you are marched down the hallway and you launch into your oratory. It is perhaps the finest speech of your life, using logical and emotional appeals that would bring tears to the eyes of even the most evil of humans. You begin at the source of all conflict—the lack of compassion and cooperation that is a plague upon sentience—and work your way to the specifics—or what you can muster, which is very little—of the present conflict between gnomes and goblins.

The guards laugh, and soon one runs off and returns with a second band, so they too can hear you and be amused.

They speak amongst themselves in a language you can't understand, and you're led into an underground zoo, a terrible menagerie full of creatures that, like you, can only suffer if denied sunlight.

A cage is opened, and you're thrown in. The only other occupant is a pile of bones and the dry-rotted garb of a mime.

In addition to the mighty lion, the fearsome golden eagle, and the ponderous sloth, there are cages holding creatures you've never set eyes upon, many of which walk upright and wear clothing. But none speak to you.

You scour your cage for a way out, to no avail. You scream, just once, a catharsis that rattles the cages and wakes all the creatures sleeping in the place, and then you sit down, once again, to drink yourself into a stupor.

At some point, a guard comes and makes your position clear. You are to be displayed as a pacifist, the most rare and least capable of nature's creatures. You will be well fed, cared for, and drugged at your wish. But only as long as you continue to orate.

It's up to you, dear reader, how you spend the rest of your time in that terrible cage, a league beneath the surface of the earth. Will you play their jester and amuse them, eating fine steaks and drinking absinthe? Or will you starve yourself out of pride? Will you go mad? Madder than you are? Or will you adapt, somehow, and attempt to make company with the few gnomes who visit the dusty, cruel cave that holds you?

No matter what you choose, you have reached

**The End**

### Thirty-Five

"So, do you actually have a plan? Or are you just going to charge at the city gates, me swinging my cane?" you ask.

"I've got some leverage I've been thinking about," he responds.

"Good enough for me," you say. "Brandy?"

You pull a flask from your boot and the two of you make short work of it. Your vision adequately blurred, your movements pleasantly fluid, and your brain somewhere taking a nap, the two of you pull open the steel gates and work your way through narrow service tunnels.

You crawl on your hands and knees, until A'gog convinces you to stand up. It turns out that the ceiling is actually above your head, despite what your drunken mind had convinced you.

Eventually, you find your way to an underground menagerie, a bizarre zoo filled with sad creatures.

"Here's the plan," A'gog explains. "We set the lion loose, and wait for someone to come by. Then, while they're busy fighting the lion, we steal their keys or take them hostage or do something else that seems clever like make a gnome-suit from their skin."

"Of course," you say, because there isn't too much else that one could say to such a proposition. "Just one question. Why won't the lion eat *us* if we set it free?"

"Aren't you British?" A'gog asks.

"Well, by birth, though certainly not by allegiance."

"Can't you Brits stare lions into submission? I thought it was part of, you know, your deal."

"I have no idea what you're talking about."

"Well you climb up onto that one," A'gog points at an empty cage that's decorated like an 18th century French bedroom, "and I'll just ride the lion. Lions don't eat goblins."

His logic impeccable in your altered state, you clamber up the cage after only three failed attempts. A'gog enters the lion cage and mounts the beast as though it were a horse (or, for size comparison, an elephant). And you set about to wait.

It's not long—well, maybe it's long, but you're drunk so you don't really know—before a gaggle of gnomish children wander into the zoo.

"Now," A'gog yells, and bursts out of the cage, barreling down on the hapless kids.

*To jump down into the midst of your foes, cane swinging, go to* **Forty-Five** *(page 76).*

*To argue that the gnomes are only children, and should not be slain or even injured, go to* **Fifty-One** *(page 84).*

## Thirty-Six

"I think what we need right now is a good rabble-rousing. A speech. That'll test the waters, and we'll find out soon enough what the kabouters are made of."

"We're made of carbon, same as a human."

"It's a metaphor."

"No, a metaphor is when you say one thing is another. Like 'kabouters muscles are mushrooms and their brains are nightmares.'"

"What?"

"I'm not certain. I think we are both speaking the same language, but yet we are not speaking the same language, yes?"

"Well, my name is Gregory," you say, and stick out your hand.

"And mine is Sergei," he says.

Russian indeed. Quite curious.

"Now, Gregory, let us go into Underburg—as you no doubt have heard it called—and I will gather up everyone who will listen at the… the best word is 'church.' And then you will be disappointed when no one joins your glorious revolution but me and one or two of my friends."

You hand A'gog the light, and begin to descend the ladder. A'gog caps the lighter and joins you. You climb in darkness.

You count one hundred rungs or so before you are too distracted by the creepy, echoing shrieks that bounce throughout the darkness about you. It seems forever before your foot touches the floor. You stand and stretch to your full height, your bones creaking, your muscles sore, and you've a bit of a headache coming on. Then A'gog's foot is on your head, then his whole weight, and the two of you drop to the ground.

"Sorry about that. Thought you was the ground."

"I'm not the ground," you say.

"Well I know that *now*."

"Mind striking a flame?" you ask, as you get to your feet.

"I do mind, matter of fact. It's a bad idea."

"Why? I thought no one here can see? What'll it matter?"

"This whole city is pretty flammable, and the kabouters don't like fire."

Suddenly, you hear a screech right next to your head, disorienting you. You realize, of course, that it is just Sergei getting a sense of his surroundings.

"Follow me," the kabouter says, and grabs your elbow. You reach back and grab A'gog by the hair, and the three of you traipse off into the invisible city. Well, it's not really invisible, of course. You just can't see it. By that standard, you're invisible too.

Sergei calls out in a language that sounds like Yankee, if Yankees spoke gibberish, and you hear at least a dozen voices respond.

"They're gathering," he says.

"I'll interpret," A'gog says to you. "I like interpreting. Only thing I'm good for, really."

You try to think of something to raise his spirits, but you really don't know the first thing about him except that he's old, he's a goblin, and he's small as hell. And that he likes alcohol.

"Want a sip of gin?" you ask, offering him a flask you had strapped to your shin under the cuff of your pants.

"Of course," he says. "Now, what are you going to talk about?"

"Oh, that."

*To give a speech about how cruel the gnomes are for how they treat the kabouters, about how oppressed the members of the middle class are, go to* **Fifty-Four** *(page 86).*

*To instead appeal to them as powerful folks who can lay their privilege on the line to aid the poor goblins, go to* **Fifty** *(page 82).*

### Thirty-Seven

"You know, I've had a really great evening, all told, and have learned quite so much, but I'm afraid it's getting quite early and a gentleman must have his rest, you see."

A'gog looks at you, and nods. "Coward, then. Fair enough. I suppose it's not your fight, now is it? I suppose you can live quite happily on the surface of the world, sunlight on your face, free from the government of your birth but not the despots of your adopted country, no reason to be bothered by the agony that we slaves suffer right beneath your feet. You wouldn't be the first."

"Quite right," you say, "I'm so glad you understand! Now, if you could be so kind as to direct me back to my tower? I quite look forward to sleeping."

But rather than answer you, A'gog pries the steel doors open a crack and disappears through.

You leave him to his fate and count on your sense of direction to lead you home.

Eight hours later, at the edge of desperation, you stumble up the stairs to your tower, trigger the secret door, and collapse on the floor of the tower's entryway. The door slams shut behind you, and you pass out, sober and exhausted.

"Wake up," you hear, and you look up to see the face of a young woman.

"I had the craziest dream," you say, "and I must have sleep-walked down the steps…"

"I don't care about your dream. I have a message for you," she speaks in clear English with a French accent.

"A message?" you say, excited. You like messages. "Is it from some attractive person who wishes to make the acquaintance of a man of words such as I?"

The woman's boot finds your face, bloodying your nose. "Don't fuck with the gnomes. The gnomes will fucking kill you, and they'll find your brother and they'll kill him too."

The woman leaves you, stalking away, and you rise to a sitting position.

You don't like being bullied, and you don't like to be struck outside the bedroom.

You sell your possessions and buy a pistol. The goblins know where to find you, and next time you'll be ready to help them. With absinthe to steel your will, you'll take on any foe of liberty. But first, to bust your brother out of prison in the colonies. No matter, you've a friend who can help you stow away. The future will be bright, bloody, and drunk, you determine. And full of freedom.

**The End**

## Thirty-Eight

"So you kabouters are slaves, when it comes down to it?"

"Of course," the kabouter says.

"But they treat you well enough, most of the time."

"Indeed, as long as we don't cause too much trouble, we don't even really know we're slaves."

"Exactly!" you say.

"Exactly what?" the kabouter asks.

"In order to free the kabouters, we need to bring down the wrath of the gnomes upon them."

"What you are saying is the opposite of sense. Perhaps you've had too much to drink? I can smell it on your breath."

"No, no... you have to understand my good... say, I didn't catch your name?"

"Sergei," the kabouter says. Russian indeed. "And you?"

"Gregory. You'll have to trust me about this. It'll work."

"Why would I trust you? I've just met you." Sergei says.

"You can trust him," A'gog says, "because he thinks he's hallucinating all of this."

"None of you make sense," Sergei says.

"Look, let's just go build some barricades, throw some rocks at gnomes. You'll see."

"Well, I do like to throw rocks at gnomes," Sergei concedes.

"It's settled," you say, as though anything were settled. You pass the lighter to A'gog and begin to descend the ladder. Soon, A'gog snuffs the flame and you climb down into a darkness filled with a silence punctuated by horrendous screeching.

You count some two hundred rungs before a screech, closer than the others, shatters your nerve. You lose count—and almost your grip—but then realize that it came from Sergei, above, and not actually from a giant, human-eating bat swooping ever nearer to you in the dark. Unless, of course, there is more to kabouters than you've currently been told.

You find the floor and set your feet down, quite excited to be on solid ground—until you remember that you're leagues beneath the surface of the earth! At the last minute, you step out of the way, realizing that others are coming down the in the dark.

"Let's cause some ruckus," A'gog says as he joins you.

"Right then. Sergei, which way to the tunnel to the gnomish city?"

"We call them hallways. And the city you speak of is called Hak'kal." He expels a good bit of phlegm with this last word.

"Something in your throat?"

"That's the city's name. Hak'kal. It's where the gnomes live. And the hall is this way. Follow me," he says, and his voice trails off in the darkness.

He leads you by talking constantly, and you learn about how the gnomes and the kabouters came to these caverns from elsewhere, hundreds of years ago, displacing the goblins into the lower depths where the mushrooms don't grow as abundantly. You learn about how the goblins make an attempt to free themselves once a generation, and that the gnomes are currently on guard for the next attempt.

"We're far enough from the rest of Underburg that you could probably use that lighter to see," Sergei says. "Actually, here." Something is thrust into your hands that feels like a wet stick. "Light this."

The lighter flares, and you realize you're holding a stick that looks like it's made of a brittle wax. "This is snot, isn't it?" you ask as A'gog sets the torch alight.

"Yup," A'gog says.

"Huh."

You're standing in a natural cavern, certainly the largest and most fantastic that you've ever seen. Everything glitters, and strange formations drip down the walls and dangle from the ceiling. The floor, however, has been leveled.

At the edge of your torchlight, you see the beginning of a city that looks like it was made by mad, gigantic bees. It's clearly more a hive than it is a distinct series of buildings, and it's a hive made of the same waxy snot as your torch.

In the other direction, there's a hallway. Looks a bit like a service hallway you would find under a modern building, with steam-pipes and all.

"Well, let's do some damage," you say.

You start grabbing rubble from the cavern and piling it, and Sergei starts cementing it together with snot.

A'gog, in the meantime, has pulled a monkey wrench out from somewhere and is going at the pipes with a single-minded determination.

It doesn't take long before you have a goblin-high wall across the corridor and the pipes and cables have been tangled into confusion.

Nor does it take long for the guards to arrive.

"Douse the light!" Sergei whispers. "I hear three gnomes coming."

You go to smother it against the rock wall, but you've forgotten that the mortar itself is combustible, and soon you stand before a burning barricade!

Now you can hear the gnomes running towards you. The three of you gather up rocks and throw them through the flames, laughing with revolutionary joy when you hear one conk off of metal that you take to be a guard's helmet. The flames are so high and thick that you cannot see, but at least the gnomes will not see you either. After several minutes of tossing rocks, you retreat.

"This way," Sergei says, and grabs you by the arm. You pick up A'gog and carry him as though he were a toddler, and run into the dark city ahead. You're led through a screeching crowd and are told to crawl into a small corridor.

"Thank you, my friends," you say to your companions, your heart full of adrenaline—finer perhaps than any drug.

"Sip of brandy, calm the nerves?" A'gog asks, uncorking a bottle and placing it into your hand.

"No thanks," you say, surprising yourself. You've no desire to dull the fervor you feel.

"What now?" Sergei asks. A fine question.

*Go to* **Forty-Six** *(page 77).*

### Thirty-Nine

But several hours go by and the gates never open, the horde never storms forward to lay siege upon the gnomish city. The crowd around you begins to murmur.

"The machine above must not have succeeded. Yi'ta must have failed."

"What does that mean?" you ask.

"That we will have to wait another six months before we can try again. Another six months of work, but another six months of training. Come on, shall we?" Gu'dal places a warm hand on the back of your knee, and the crowd in the room is beginning to drift away, out through various tunnels.

"I'm not sure," you demur. You think about your warm, lumpy bed that waits for you in your tower.

But Gu'dal gives you a look that might be what goblins use to smelt metal. "You were ready to give your life for our cause, but you aren't willing to spend six months among us, preparing?"

"When you put it that way, it does sound rather foolish," you admit. But somehow it *is* different. You prefer the thrill of adventure to the routine of labor, regardless of risk. But you suppose that life in a goblin work camp might be adventurous enough, and you steel your resolve. "Alright then, where you lead I shall follow."

You join the largest mass of goblins as they leave the large chamber, out into a new hallway. The ceiling remains a comfortably above your head by a foot or so, which you realize must seem cavernously high to the goblins.

"Gu'dal," you hear, "you simply *must* to introduce me to your British friend here." A spiky, mismatched suit of full plate armor—presumably with a goblin inside—falls into step beside you. "You are British, are you not?"

"Perhaps by birth," you reply.

"Ah! Of course. How rude of me. The name is Trevor."

"Tre'vortin," Gu'dal corrects.

"No, just Trevor will do."

This is clearly an argument that the two have had before.

"Gregory, meet Trevor. Trevor here is an Anglophile." The disdain in her voice is quite plain.

The suit of plate mail thrusts a spiked gauntlet towards you, which you look at uncertainly.

"Right," the helmet says, then two steel fists rise up and the helmet is lifted free of the armor. Underneath is a goblin fellow that you dare say is dashing, with a cute pug nose and rather kind eyes.

For the rest of your walk, Trevor regales you with tales of travel throughout the caverns of Undereurope, and Gu'dal walks silently. You're not certain, but you think she might be sulking.

Just as Trevor is explaining the nature of Scandinavian ghasts, you step out of a tunnel into a cavern the size of, well, the size of a gigantic cavern. It's lit intermittently by gaslight, and you realize that there is an entire town enclosed within.

And what a town! It is built vertically as well as horizontally, the air strung across with ropes and nets, some ropes so dense together that they form what look like nothing more than hives. Goblins of all sorts clamber along lines, swing through the air, crawl across the walls and ceiling. On the ground, the wargoblins are stripping their armor and hiding it amongst stray machinery and kitchen supplies. Many trade their armor for pickaxes and walk, no spring in their step, out into side tunnels. Back to work, you presume.

"Welcome to Haddlelint," Gu'dal says.

"Haddlelint," you repeat.

"It means 'primary goblin camp' in Gnomish," Trevor explains, then places a hand affectionately on your knee.

"Oh."

*To spend the next six months studying and training under Gu'dal, go to* **Forty-Four** *(page 74).*

*To pass most of your time having fun and drinking with Trevor, go to* **Forty-Nine** *(page 80).*

## Forty

You leave Gu'dal behind as you walk around the corner, uncertain what fate might hold in store for you. The corridor opens up into a large natural cavern, reinforced with stone-block pillars. Stalactites grin down at you, some of them held together with steel bracing. The unmistakable smell of opium smoke lingers in the air.

Before you stand two gnomes. What else could they be? They are nearly twice as tall as the goblins—their eyes reaching to your waist. You're curious to see their faces, but these two guards wear elaborate helmets that remind you of nothing so much as diver's helmets, only with dark tinted glass over their faces. Each holds a rifle of the most bizarre model you've ever seen, gleaming bright copper and brass with crystals mounted along the bore in strange configurations.

The guards are placed on either side of a set of impressive steel doors, inlaid with ornamentation in floral patterns. For a moment you are taken with the fierce desire to wake up, to return to your bedroom and your vices.

Upon seeing you, the guards aim their weapons directly at you. "*Qui êtes-vous?*" one of them, the slightly pudgy one, asks.

"I'm sorry?" you say.

"Who is there?" he—for you presume it to be a he, although you don't feel totally confident in your gender assumptions—asks.

"My name is Gregory, and I've come from above. I, uh, I'd like to speak with your leader."

The skinnier gnome nods, and turns to a voice-horn embedded into the wall beside the doors. The guard speaks in a language you don't recognize, one both guttural and rolling. It's a bit like Finnish, but with shorter words.

The guard turns his or her ear to the voice-horn, awaiting a reply, then turns back towards you. In a heavy accent, the gnome announces: "Someone will be with you shortly. If you try anything, I will shoot you with this lightrifle."

You spend a most stressful five minutes staring intently at the doors of Hak'kal. But eventually, they open. Beyond, you can see a beautiful, gaslit city. It reminds you a bit of Prague, if Prague were inhabited solely by five-year-old children. The roof of it is beyond your vision, and the chamber is so massive that you nearly believe you have returned, somehow, to the surface of the world.

Through the portal walks a self-important guard, walking like a precocious boy-soldier, his rifle swinging in one hand. You identify him as the leader with ease; a remarkable number of badges and medals (is that a political pin from Paris?) adorn the entirety of his uniform, from lapel to trouser-cuff, his bucket-helmet reveals his face and bears a two-hand-high bronze sculpture of himself.

"Yes?" His voice is gruff, and he walks up to you without fear as he speaks. He looks you over, and you can tell when he meets your eyes that he doesn't see you as much of a threat to him. Despite being twice his height, you tend to agree with this assessment.

"I will have an audience with your city's ruling body, be it monarch or parliament. I am here as ambassador from the goblins."

"Tricked you into that, did they? Well, alright. I'll ask for you. Would you like some tea, or some opium, while you wait?"

*To ask for some tea, go to* **Forty-Three** *(page 73).*

*To ask for opium, go to* **Forty-Eight** *(page 79).*

*To politely decline the offer of refreshments, go to* **Fifty-Two** *(page 85).*

## Forty-One

"What sort of vapors?" you ask, curious.

"Ether," the taller goblin says.

"Where you lead, I shall follow," you say.

And what a feat of following! You are on their spry heels for nearly two hours, navigating twisting natural caverns, at one point crawling, before you reach your destination.

Your destination is an open cave room that forms an amphitheater of sorts, bedecked in a mind-altering display of flashing color, flame, and scintillating crystals. Your mind tries in vain to form patterns in the noise, yet you seem to be unable to resist the attempt, hoping to find constellations where there just might be none.

Suddenly your attention is arrested by a booming voice quite inhuman, even quite ingoblin. "Greetings, wayfarer. Your journey has only begun." You look to the bottom of the theatre and see what might be the gauntest giant you have ever laid eyes upon. Well, you've never actually laid eyes on a giant, but you had always pictured them to be, you know, thick as well as tall. This man—and indeed his manhood is quite clearly displayed—is seven feet tall while seated (and likely, of course, twice that standing!) but as thin, if not thinner, than you.

"How'd you get in here?" you ask, annoyed for some reason. "I had to crawl, and I'm only like five foot nine. I got my clothes all muddy."

Your question seems to catch the giant off guard. "I grew up here," he says.

"You've never left this room?"

"Perhaps not in body," he says, and you try not to scoff. "But with the use of the holy *thak'narra* fungus, one can travel anywhere, for days or years at a time."

This gets your attention. Drugs you understand, even if sitting cross-legged and emaciated doesn't seem like the indulgent life you'd hoped for.

"Your journey to find peace begins in this room," he says, and a tiny goblin—perhaps a child?—comes to your foot and offers up a murky black tincture in a crystal vial.

You uncap it and swallow, excited. You sit, and for fifteen minutes you return to your attempt at tracing constellations in the lights that encircle the room. The drug kicks in, and suddenly everything makes sense. The lights merge in your consciousness, and you realize that they are not separate lights, not really. That they're all together, forming a skull. "A skull," you say, to the giant and the goblins. "A skull symbolizes life itself, a skull contains our brains and keeps our head in its proper shape! How lovely, how peaceful!"

"You saw a skull?" a voice asks, though you are no longer certain who is talking. It might be you. Or the giant. Or, of course, someone else, like God.

"Of course!" you say.

"Crap," the voice says. Would God curse? You suppose It might. You also aren't used to believing in God.

"Wait, he was British, wasn't he?" It says. You would have thought God would have known the answer to that.

"Why can't you give the British *thak'narra*?" says the voice, although It doesn't appear to be talking to you.

"The British are human, you realize," God says to Itself.

"Really? Oh. Oh crap," God replies.

Then you die.

**The End**

### Forty-Two

You'll never know if it was cowardice or reason that drove you to do it, but you throw your hands into the air and take a step back. "I've no idea what I've gotten myself into," you announce.

Gu'dal turns and looks at you, a vile, malicious look that might well keep you awake at night the rest of your days. But as her back is turned, the gnome steps forward and brings a blackjack down on the back of her skull, knocking her top hat onto the pavement. Gu'dal crumbles in its wake.

"You've done the right thing," the gnome tells you. "Now go get drunk, you louse."

With something like guilt and something like the relief of oblivion, you journey into an all-night bar to take the gnome's sarcastic advice.

When you return home the next noon, you stumble upon a tripwire set across your threshold. As your face hits the floor, you hear a sad laugh and your life comes to an immediate end.

### The End


### Forty-Three

The captain walks back towards the voice-horn and shouts a series of unintelligible commands into it. He then turns and smiles at you, his teeth white and straight and, unlike the goblins', protruding from gums as pink as your own.

A few moments later, two fairly small gnomes come through the gates, bearing a fine silver tray with a china tea set between the two of them. One of the cups is human-sized, and this is filled for you. The wonderful aroma of tea leaves fills the chamber.

You sit cross-legged upon the ground and sip at the cup, relaxing quite a bit. How civil these gnomes are, you think.

*Go to* **Fifty-Eight** *(page 92).*

## Forty-Four

You're shown to a human-sized cot in a shadowy corner of the cavern, far from any side tunnels and obscured by layers and layers of net. "The gnomes won't know that you're here," Gu'dal explains, "because if they find you, they'll take you away."

It's with that ominous warning that you begin your time in Haddlelint. The goblins here keep time by the brightness of their lamps; each is controlled by a central clockwork that shuts off or dims them at night, slowly bringing them to full-bright at noon. There are no other timepieces, but you learn to adjust.

You're woken early each morning by a now-playful Gu'dal, who sometimes dumps water on your head, sometimes yells Goblin obscenities in your ear. You're led off down side tunnels—chosen so as to avoid gnomish observation—and she teaches you the rudiments of cane-fighting.

Despite outweighing her perhaps six times over, she wallops you soundly for three months before you are able to hold your own.

"Remember," she says one day as you practice, "if a rifle-gnome points her lightrifle at you, dodge left. Always left. It works more often than right."

Then, at noon each day, Gu'dal leaves for her work shift and you hide in the main room. Most often, you play tiles with the goblins, who have dozens—if not hundreds—of drinking games that you explore.

But you find yourself drinking less than you had on the surface, certainly no more than two flasks a day. Which is not to say that the goblin sugar-mushroom brandy isn't good. It is. You just find yourself taken by this new sense of self, this image of yourself as a warrior.

And when Gu'dal returns in the evenings, and the two of you take long walks through the tunnels, you find yourself more and more taken with her. Five months into your stay, you're physically fit, practically sober (no more than six shots in an evening!), and quite resoundingly in love with your mentor, who is almost two feet tall and has claws for fingernails.

She seems fond of you as well. No longer does she wake you with sharp jabs in the underside of your ribs. Rather, she licks your cheek, or bounces on your chest as though it were a trampoline. One morning she walks alongside you on stilts, then places her arm around your waist. You nearly faint with happiness.

Six months pass faster than you realized could be possible, and it is the last night before the horde gathers once more. You sit with Gu'dal, perched on a net forty feet from the cavern floor, and stare at the stalactites above, imagining constellations in their patterns. You pull the silver ring out of your pocket, and consider what to do.

*To ask Gu'dal to elope with you, afraid that if you fight you might lose one another, go to* **Fifty-Seven** *(page 92).*

*To offer the ring as a good luck charm and go valiantly towards battle and death, go to* **Sixty-One** *(page 97).*

## Forty-Five

You leap from your perch, and fortunately a small child breaks your fall. You spin about in all directions, everything a blur, and strike about randomly.

Screams fill the air and bring bloodlust into your eyes. The lion rends, your cane bludgeons, and soon all of your foes are subdued.

The lion peacefully laps at blood that pools on the floor, and A'gog looks pleased. The bodies of almost a dozen gnomes are scattered about.

"We should get out of here," you say, because you're afraid you might vomit if you let yourself think about what you've done.

"Oh, no. No, we won't be going anywhere. More will come, and more shall fall. The great evil city of Hak'kal will be up-rooted like... like if you were to cut the tendrils off a moss. We shall be victorious!"

Suddenly, three grown gnomes run into the room, wielding complex and bizarre rifles—adorned with crystals that spin and throw specks of light across the chamber—and wearing full-face helmets covered with darkened glass.

You don't think—you're far too drunk on adrenaline and booze for that—but instead rush them, your cane raised.

A purple beam shoots out and glances against your chest, stinging, but you bring your cane down on the faceplate of the gnome who shot you and break glass into his face, destroying his eyes. Soon you're joined by A'gog and his lion, and a second guard falls. The third runs.

You make to chase the fleeing figure, but A'gog stops you. "Let them run," he says, "let them tell the whole city that we are here."

"We're not going to win this, are we?"

"No," A'gog says, "but they'll pay for my life of slavery. I thank you, stranger, for giving yourself to this."

"Yeah, well, I kinda thought I was hallucinating it all."

A'gog nods. You pull a final flask from your back pocket, and you drain it.

More guards will come. And you will die. But at least you'll die in some weird cavern far underground, miles from where you were born, on a grand and twisted adventure, with no ethics to speak of. At least you will die free.

Nevertheless, you will die.

### The End

### Forty-Six

"What do we have to work with?" you ask.

"We've got the three of us," Sergei says. "And we've got a lot of angry kabouters who may or may not help us."

"That's not a lot," A'gog says.

"Well it's more than we had on our way here, now isn't it?" you reply. You've come down from your adrenaline high, but the fervor of fomenting revolution has gone to your head, and nothing seems impossible.

"What better time to start putting up propaganda? The kabouters are going to be mad at the gnomes anyway," Sergei says.

"That's useless," A'gog replies, "we don't need words, we need action. And besides, I hate to break it to you, but you can't read. You're blind."

You hear a slap in the dark, and realize that Sergei has struck A'gog. "We've been reading and writing with our fingers since before you goblins figured out steam!"

"That's enough," you say, but no one is actually listening to you.

"Alright, alright, I'm sorry. I sometimes think stupid things, and sometimes I say them. But still, we don't need words. We need action. You kabouters have got your own police force, yeah? That keeps tabs on the rebels and reports to Hak'kal?"

"Yes," Sergei says, suddenly quite subdued.

"So we kill them. With poison. Poison is good for killing people who are bigger than you when you don't have guns."

"Maybe," Sergei says, "maybe."

*To throw your weight behind the idea of disseminating propaganda throughout Underburg, go to* **Sixty-Two** *(page 98).*

*To support political assassination, go to* **Fifty-Five** *(page 87).*


## Forty-Seven

You look at Gu'dal and you look at the gnome. Never an unduly handsome man yourself, you reach the conclusion that, right or wrong, you will side with the goblins.

Gu'dal catches your eye, and a smile crosses both of your faces simultaneously. Her sword comes free of her cane and before you've time to think she has cut the hamstrings of one of the policemen.

You lunge forward, catching the gendarme closest to you in the chin with your club with a lucky blow. The gnome latches his jaws onto your right thigh and jabs at your left with what seems to be nothing other than a beartrap on a stick. You stumble, unable to control your legs, and collapse onto the ground. A cop leers above you and you swing wildly with your cane, smacking quietly into his grinning mouth.

He spits blood and you pass out.

When you come to, you're in a nearby alley with smelling salts under your nose. "You did great!" Gu'dal tells you.

"I feel it," you say, lying. You look at your legs. Both have vicious wounds and you doubt you'll be running or fighting again soon. "I would have thought that gnomes wouldn't have such sharp teeth."

"They don't," Gu'dal says, "they're herbivores. But they also eat rocks."

With the help of your cane—no longer an affectation but a necessity—you find your way to your feet. You can support your own weight, if barely.

"Thank you for," Gu'dal says, "you know–"

"It's nothing," you say. "Never liked cops anyway."

Gu'dal grins and you find your way to the next tower slowly, but without further interruptions.

*Go to* **Fifty-Six** *(page 89).*


## Forty-Eight

The captain shouts something through the voice-horn, then smiles at you. His teeth are white and straight, you realize, with gums as pink as your own. An herbivore's—or at least an omnivore's—smile. You can't help but find it somewhat comforting.

A few moments later the great city gates open and a gnome walks out bearing an opium pipe, which he or she—you are really having a hard time distinguishing gnomish genders—sets down in front of you and lights with a coal.

The flowery taste of opium floods into your lungs and you begin to relax. These gnomes can't be all bad, you decide. Until you remember your brother's lecture to you, about how western imperialists pushed poppy addiction upon the places they conquered as a way to keep the colonized subservient.

Still, you're glad to be smoking.

*Go to* **Fifty-Eight** *(page 92).*

## Forty-Nine

You're led to a cot only a few inches too short for you hidden in a dark corner of the cavern, obscured from view by a thick canopy of netting.

"Here, the gnomes won't see you. Your presence will be a secret," Trevor tells you. "Now, drink this."

You take the proffered ceramic bottle and smell it. Clearly alcohol, and potent. You drink. It burns your tongue and your throat in that lovely, lovely way that tastes like home.

"What is this," you ask.

"Sweet-mushroom brandy," Trevor replies. "Let's get drunk."

And with such prophetic words, you begin your stay in Haddlelint. Every morning, you're roused by Trevor playing drums upon your breast. You drink your breakfast and usually set into one of their seemingly hundreds of games that use tiles as pieces, then find some sort of menial task to help with for an hour or so, like washing dishes or chopping mushrooms. The other gnomes, including Gu'dal, spend most of their time out in the mines, departing at all hours with pickaxe and bucket.

"Why don't you work?" you ask Trevor one day, early into your stay.

"Why don't you?" Trevor replies.

"Because the gnomes don't even know I'm here," you say.

"Nor me," Trevor grins. "I escaped years ago, when I went off to travel the world. They've got me down as 'fugitive, presumed dead' in their charts. I came back because there's nowhere finer. But who would want to work if they don't have to?"

"Fair enough," you nod. "But how do you eat?"

"My brethren would never let me starve, oh no! They feed me from their share, and I do what I can to help. And I'm here as a soldier. I think that, really, that gets me off the hook... being ready to die to fight against the gnomes and all."

You're not sure you believe him, but since you're in a similar position, you don't say anything more of it.

For six months you learn all sorts of things about the caverns all across Undereurope. For instance, you learn that goblins are herbivores—fungivores, really—and have sharp teeth so as to break down the cell walls of the mushrooms they eat so that they can get all of the protein.

You learn about goblin music, too. In goblin music theory, the size and shape of the chamber you are in matters as much to the song as the melody, so one set of words sung in one room is an entirely different song than one sung in another!

You learn about goblin art and literature, about poetry, about drinking and games like "spike in your knee" and "net hoppers" and "dodge-rock" (the last being too literal for your tastes). You don't learn much about fighting.

But you do learn a bit about love. The more time you spend with Trevor, the closer you feel. You begin to stray farther and farther into the underwilds, often staying away from Haddlelint for days at a time, foraging your meals. When away from civilization, Trevor stays sober. And, miraculously, so do you. You laugh and write stories together, imagining fantastical adventures that sit atop the real adventure that you are on.

You tell him about your family, about your flight from England to join your brother, about your brother's deportation to the prison colony. You cry in the small, green man's arms, and, yes, fall in love.

Six months pass so swiftly that it startles you. Suddenly, it is the night before the re-gathering of the horde, of the attack upon Hak'kal. You sit with Trevor at the edge of an underground pool, staring at the untroubled waters in front of you.

You pull the silver ring from your coat pocket, and fumble with it in your hands.

*To ask Trevor to elope with you, to go explore the wilds of the underworld and ne'er return, go to* **Fifty-Nine** *(page 96).*

*To hand Trevor the ring, in hopes that it brings him luck in the next day's battle, go to* **Sixty-Four** *(page 100).*

## Fifty

You hear the shrieks of more kabouters, and by the sound of the footsteps you guess that hundreds must be gathering to listen to you speak. Eventually, A'gog gives you the cue.

"My fellows," you begin, and A'gog interprets. "My fellows, I come here to beg you. To appeal to your might."

You turn towards A'gog. "Er, I know they enslave goblins, but what do they do to humans?"

"They put you in a cage above the city of Hak'kal and make you sing for your supper."

"And 'Hak'kal,' that's the name of the city? And not just you clearing your throat?"

"Yes."

"Thanks," you say, then turn back to address the crowd. "In Hak'kal I might be caged and forced to sing, for no reason but my height and my birth. Is this a decent thing?"

The crowd answers, and A'gog tells you: "They admit that's not the best thing that's ever happened."

"I came below the surface because I met a goblin, A'gog here, who cares about the welfare of his people. The goblins, they are hard workers. Perhaps as hard of workers as yourselves. But the goblins aren't given the sparing bits of freedom afforded to you; they toil with the eyes of guards upon them at every moment."

The crowd murmurs. "One admits that this isn't any good, but another, bastard, says that we goblins are lazy and useless and we wouldn't work if the guards weren't constantly threatening us."

"I don't know if that's true," you say. "Who wants to work on other people's projects? I mean, who likes to work, to labor? And down here, the goblins, under guard at every moment, cannot free themselves. The humans, caged above Hak'kal, cannot free themselves. Will the gnomes free the goblins, the humans? Yourselves?"

Just as you begin to warm to your subject, a light appears in the distance, growing quickly. Kabouters scream and throw themselves into a panic, most scattering to all directions. You feel a cold hand take yours and find yourself dragged away, stumbling in the dark.

More noises, chaos, and distant lights, and you find yourself in a small tunnel, most likely another ventilation corridor. You hear A'gog beside you, cursing softly under his breath in French. Then Sergei speaks up:

"The gnomes must have heard us gathering; we weren't expecting them for another week at least." He pauses for a moment. "I liked what you had to say. But even with your fancy speeches, you'll find no help among the kabouters. We're well fed and left alone and most us don't even know we are slaves. Even now, when the gnomes will beat us for gathering, most kabouters will simply blame my friends and I for allowing it to happen."

"Well, thanks for getting us out of there."

"It is nothing to risk oneself for the cause of emancipation. I must tell you, however, that your gnome friend here was a bit creative in his translations of your speech. I didn't hear you use the phrases 'glorious worker's utopia' or 'communist state under the dictatorship of the proletariat.'"

"Hey, English is like my fourth language," A'gog replies, "okay? I just got flustered with so many people listening. Let's have some brandy, yeah? I mean, we're alive at least, we got away from those stupid flat-toothed guards, didn't we?"

You hear the sound of bottle uncorking and feel the drink put into your hands. "Not right now," you say, surprising yourself. "We need to figure out what to do."

*Go to* **Forty-Six** *(page 77).*


## Fifty-One

"Wait," you shout, and A'gog halts his steed in mid-stride. "We can't kill them!"

"What? Why not?"

While you're talking, the children scatter, most running back out the way that they came, a few running deeper into the chamber.

"Because they're children," you say.

"Right!" A light goes on in the drunken fog of your friend's mind. "Children! Children make *great* hostages!"

Suddenly, two children make a break past you for the exit.

*To grab the kid on the left, go to* **Sixty** *(page 97).*

*To grab the kid on the right, go to* **Sixty-Five** *(page 101).*

*To let the kids go by, go to* **Sixty-Three** *(page 100).*


### Fifty-Two

The captain shrugs—a decidedly human gesture—and smiles at you. You notice that his gums are as pink as your own and that his teeth are decidedly non-carnivorous, something that puts you slightly at ease.

He walks over to the voice-horn and shouts something un-intelligible through it, something that sounds fairly angry.

You stand uncomfortably for about five minutes before any-thing else of note transpires.

*Go to* **Fifty-Eight** *(page 92).*


### Fifty-Three

"You're listening to a gnome!" you shout at the gendarmes.

"*Je ne parler pas anglais,*" one of them replies.

"Oh, hell," you say, your options growing quite limited.

*To turn Gu'dal over to the gendarmes, go to* **Forty-Two** *(page 73).*

*To fight, go to* **Forty-Seven** *(page 78).*

## Fifty-Four

You hear hundreds of pairs of feet closing in around you as people gather, and eventually, you are given the cue to speak.

"My fellow sentient creatures," you announce.

"What does 'sentient' mean?" A'gog asks.

"Er... my fellow smart creatures," you say, and A'gog translates into Kabouter.

"What's the name of the gnomish city?" you ask A'gog.

But A'gog translates your question into Kabouter as though it were part of your speech, and the crowd answers "Hak'kal."

"Right then. The city of Hak'kal was built on top of dead kabouters. Every building crafted by unpaid labor, every brick held in place by snot mined of your noses. The history of the Hak'kal is the history of your enslavement!" You yell this with fervor, warming to the subject, and A'gog translates.

Several kabouters shout back at you. "They say that they are happy to help the gnomes, because the gnomes gave them the cave for Underburg. The kabouters are stupid," A'gog translates and interprets.

"The gnomes gave you a city so that they could exploit you!" The kabouters yell back.

"I don't think this is working. I don't think they understand the consequences of their bourgeois sympathies," A'gog informs you.

Just then, a speck of light appears in the distance, growing rapidly. The kabouters yell out as though they were one being, shrieking like some demon from the pages of a penny-dreadful. The lights get close and blind you. Clammy hands hold you.

When your eyes finally adjust, you see a single gnomish guard surrounded by wide-eyed kabouters, all of whom point with pale fingers at A'gog and yourself.

The gnome speaks to A'gog, who spits against the guard's face-shield. The guard then turns to you and speaks English. "You have been judged as a liar, a man who disturbs the peace of Hak'kal. As a creature of the surface world, you have no rights and will have no trial. You are to be garroted."

You attempt to break free, but the grip of the kabouters is too strong. You are forced to your knees, and the guard chokes the life out of you with a thin bit of rope.

### The End

### Fifty-Five

"A'gog might be right," you weigh in, "we don't need propaganda on the walls, we need propaganda of the deed. A poison plot is called for, I think, and serves two purposes: one, we kill the police who are reporting on us to Hak'kal; and two, we show people that resistance is possible, that our enemies are vulnerable. That we can fight, that we can win."

"I believe you," Sergei says. "I'm convinced. I've spent my entire adult life skulking around in the silence, waiting for something, *anything*, to happen so that I could join in, so that I could be useful, that I could advance the cause of freedom. But maybe what I need is to make that thing happen myself."

For a moment, you're struck by *déjà vu* and think you're speaking to Anton, the Russian man with whom your brother fled for France. Of course, it's partly the accent, but it's also the words. He spoke that way. And since you can't see your companion…

"Very well," you say, trying to forget that when your brother went down this path, he ended up deported to the prison colonies.

"I'll secure poison tomorrow," Sergei says. "The day after, I'll slip it into the officers' morning tea."

"What will we do," you ask.

"You two? You two are going to be my bodyguards. If anyone starts anything, you light a torch and we fight our way to freedom."

"Do you think it will work?" A'gog asks.

"Sure," Sergei says. "You two know how to fight, don't you?"

You don't have the heart to tell him the truth.

The details determined, you set about to sleep in the ventilation tunnel. You sleep lightly, tormented by dreams of gnomes (terrible monsters in your dreams, indeed as ugly as your goblin and kabouter companions) and the fear of a prison deep beneath the earth. Quite rational dreams.

When you awake, you're surprised to note that you're still underground, and not asleep in your bedchamber as you suspected.

"Good morning," A'gog says. "Have some water?"

"Thanks," you say, taking a bottle pressed into your hand in the dark. "How did you know I was awake?"

"You stopped snoring," he laughs. "I was afraid you'd give us away, but Sergei assured me... let's see, how did he put it? He said that the tunnel was like a dark place to the seeing. There's so much white noise with the air and the vents and such that it's hard to hear into. But I think he said that because he snored too. Maybe even worse than you."

"Alright," you say, and you spend that day waiting in utter darkness. For a horrible hour, you fear insanity might set in. Then you realize that indeed, you're still talking to a goblin, so it's quite likely that insanity has *already* set in, and you just decide to run with it.

Some hours later, Sergei returns to your encampment. "All is ready," he says. "Tomorrow morning, my friends will open the doors to the officers' quarters. We will go in, poison them, and escape. If anything goes wrong, you two will overpower our assailants. Be careful with your torch, though. Touch it to the wrong wall, or light it under a low ceiling, and we'll all die in flames and suffocation."

"Right," you say, because you're so scared that you cannot find more words than that. You don't want to die in the dark any way that you look at it: you don't want to burn or suffocate or be torn asunder by pasty bat-person hands. You'd much rather poison some officials, liberate some populations of strange critters, then return to your writing enriched for the effort.

The second night you don't dream. You sleep lightly, your thoughts driven by a strong sense of purpose. Your fellows awaken, you straighten your clothes, and head off into the blackness, following Sergei's footsteps. It's easier than you think to follow sounds in the dark, a dark you've nearly grown used to, but you still bump into slimy walls and the occasional offended kabouter as you make your way through the city.

"We're here," Sergei says, and a heavy gate creaks open.

*To suggest that you would be more useful outside the gates, where you could use your torch if need be, go to* **Seventy-Six** *(page 114).*

*To follow Sergei into the officer's quarters, go to* **Seventy-Eight** *(page 116).*

## Fifty-Six

The second clock tower is a domed, baroque thing about six stories in height, clearly abandoned. Both the minute and the hour hands hang slack, pointing to the roman VI, and the shutters are pulled tight and locked. Gu'dal picks the four padlocks on the door as you nervously keep guard.

Then, with an alarming groan, the door opens. The inside of the building is a single open room, with only scaffolding providing access to the clock mechanics and bells above. And it is on this scaffolding that you see the most bizarre creature you've yet seen during this strange and long night. It is half your height, pasty-white with enormous, unseeing eyes, and has hairy, overlarge ears—the lobes of which rest upon the thing's shoulders. It looks like a hyperbolic caricature of an old man. And it appears to occupy the tower alone.

It shrieks twice in rapid succession, a painfully high-pitched cry, and drops nimble as an acrobat to the floor to stand in front of you.

Gu'dal and the tower's denizen immediately break into an excited conversation in a language you can't follow. The words sound almost Finnish; in fact it could *be* Finnish for all you know of the language.

You pass the time with sips of Fernet Stock—a lovely and bitter liquor from the Kingdom of Bohemia—and by shadowboxing a reenactment of your fight with the gendarmes. You sip more heavily each time, and soon you begin to believe in your own bravery and battle-prowess, despite your wounded leg.

By the time that Gu'dal and the strange creature are through with their conversation, you are so thoroughly soused that you cannot distinguish your eyeballs from your elbows. You collapse on your way out the door.

You come to back in the belfry of your own clock tower, once more roused by smelling salts. You're still quite drunk, but you're drunk to that comfortable level you prefer to spend most of your days at, where your words and balance only occasionally fail you and your courage never does.

Yi'ta stands above you, smiling. "Well done," he says. "I hear our plans would not be going forth without you."

"What happens now?" you ask.

"We attack. In less than half an hour, our machines on the surface will shatter the front gates of Hak'kal—and, I suppose, about a city block of this city up here. The main force of our infantry will march in through the gates and be joined by the gnomish resistance movement within the city. Up here, our job will be to contain those gnomes who attempt to escape. Those who surrender to us will stand trial, and most will be pardoned. But Hak'kal must be destroyed. The colonization of our caverns will end, as will slavery. We goblins have a saying, 'Let us have one last time of bloodshed and be done with it.'"

*To say, "Of course you have a saying about that. How many times have you said it? When has it been true? No, you must abandon your plans of terror and revolution. I won't let you take so many lives, nor let you destroy an entire city block," go to* **Sixty-Six** *(page 102).*

*To say, "I volunteer my body for your cause. My brother fought for the Paris commune, and I'd be proud to fight for the emancipation of your people," go to* **Seventy-One** *(page 107).*

*To say, "You need to control the escape of the gnomes onto the surface, do you? Well I've got an idea. It involves a hot-air balloon, some guns, and a spyglass," go to* **Seventy-Five** *(page 113).*

## Fifty-Seven

"Oh Gregory," Gu'dal weeps when you present her the ring and your plan, "it's as though you don't know me at all!"

When she says this, you begin to sob.

"I can't abandon my fellow goblins. I have to fight. I live only to fight against the gnomes. I thought you understood that!"

But clearly you hadn't. Broken-hearted, you climb down from the net and return to your cot.

You don't sleep well. In the morning, you join the horde. You chant and you scream, but the blood thirst escapes you.

The steel doors open, and you rush forward, through tunnels and into the waiting lightrifles of the gnomes. You want only to die. You want Gu'dal to know you died in defense of the goblin cause.

You get your wish.

### The End

### Fifty-Eight

After several minutes, twenty guards come marching through the gates and, along with the captain, escort you into Hak'kal.

As you first walk through the gate, you realize the inadequacy of your previous comparison: Hak'kal puts Prague to shame. Here, *every* building bears a clock as complex and impressive as Prague's famed astronomical clock—and every bit as indecipherable to the layperson! Some aspects of the clock faces seem to move at the speed of frightened rabbits, while others might not have moved since the day of your birth. Each clock is strikingly unique and strikingly handsome. The buildings are striking as well. In fact, it is quite something that you are not immediately bludgeoned into unconsciousness, considering how often you are struck by this city!

The architecture is ornate, in the high gothic. Buttresses fly out from tall, stone-block houses while other buildings appear to be carved out of the very earth and, thusly solid, require no such reinforcement.

From above, you hear the clear sound of a remarkable choir, singing in—and you are both stunned by and certain of this—German! You cannot see the source, but suspect the presence of massive victrolas, developed past anything available on the surface. So remarkable, then, that they reproduce the work of Brahms!

One foot in front of the other, you sleepwalk towards the center of the city, escorted by a score of riflegnomes, led at the fore by the strange figure of the captain. What a marvelous tale you will be able to spin upon your rousing, you think.

Until suddenly, it occurs to you that the gnomes and goblins might be real and not merely be figments of your powerful and drunken mind. The reality seeps in, as does your responsibility to Gu'dal, to the goblins who are mad at work building some crazed rescue device in the tower above the ground, the tower in which you reside.

That sort of makes the goblins your allies. And yet, the gnomes are every bit so civilized! Brahms! From the ceiling and sky!

Beams of light cut through the air above you and bounce around the sides of buildings so that the city, while illuminated by gas-flame, glows in bright hues quite unfamiliar and marvelous. Everywhere around you, you see construction and activity. The miniature citizens of this city are working at a feverish pace to heighten buildings, tighten valves, ascend ladders into the darkness above, run pipe and wire, and align crystals.

Even the children seem hard at work, with all of the grins and laughter one would associate with play. There are no taskmasters, no weapons. The only pugilists are the ones who surround you.

The guards escort you to a building that appears as a miniature cathedral. Fortunately, what seems massive to a gnome is sized well for your stature, and you fit through the doorway without stooping. There is no door in the entryway to the structure, and you suddenly understand that one is not necessary. The city is impregnable from external attack, and must be—you assume—situated on some kind of thermal vent, because the weather is as pleasant as a summer's eve. (Indeed, a summer not in England, but a real summer, the likes they have on the mainland and in the colonies.)

Inside is a hallway, much like the tunnel you first explored on your way to the city, brimming with steam pipes, steam pipe accessories, gadgets, and gadget accessories.

"You will stay here this evening. You are not free to wander," a guard tells you.

You are led past multiple doors, each a plain and solid sheet of steel, before one is opened and you, with a lightrifle suddenly pressed squarely against your back, step inside what you now presume to be your cell. The door slams behind you.

This cell, however, is outfitted far finer than any hotel you might have hoped to stay at aboveground. There is a wardrobe, sink, toilet, bidet, and bed. The window is open to the outside, lacking glass or bars.

You think to escape, but promptly collapse, having been up for an untold number of hours—one that clearly exceeds your usual twenty—and are roused only by a good, solid shaking of your shoulders some time later.

You come to your senses, or at least to a fuzzy facsimile of them, and see a gnome standing above you, a man of uncommon beauty. He has ear-length hair that is unmistakably the color of copper, truly metallic and shiny, with eyes of brass and skin as pale as silver.

"We have not much, in the way of…" the gnome's accent is nearly unintelligible, but you gather that he is searching for a word.

"Time?" you suggest.

"I don't know," he replies.

You sit up and find your jacket hung from a bedpost then pull your pocket watch—still quite broken—from its pocket. You open it and show him the clock.

"Yes! Yes! We have not much in the way of time!"

"Well I'm glad that is settled, because I was afraid we might not have much in the way of wormwood." You sit up properly and begin to rub your eyes.

"I don't understand," the gnome says.

"Pardon. It's nothing. Please go on."

"We have not much time and you need to help us, help the gnome Aboveground. We want free the goblins from the tyranny, cruelty, despotism of Ji'ka!" For lacking a complete grammar, the gnome has a remarkable political vocabulary.

Your eyes well rubbed, you double-check. Sure enough, the short man in front of you is indeed a gnome, and not a goblin. Square teeth, green-less skin, comes higher than your knees.

"Alright," you say, because there's not so much that you can really say to such a request. "How may I be of service?"

"Your actions are your own. There is a word in Gnomish, and in English it is perhaps... autonomy. Free will. We are not your Gods. You can join us, fight with us. Or you can want your audience, and study information for us."

"And if I refuse to help? If I side with the council of Hak'kal?"

"Then tomorrow we will kill you. You will not study us to them."

Free will appears to have its limits.

*To inform him that you are here to act as an ambassador for the goblins, and intend to seek resolution by means of words, go to* **Sixty-Seven** *(page 103).*

*To escape your cell through the open window and join the gnomish Aboveground, go to* **Seventy-Two** *(page 109).*

*To verbally express your discontent with the gnomish Aboveground's threats upon your health, then shout for your guard to capture the interloper, go to* **Seventy-Seven** *(page 115).*

#### Fifty-Nine

Trevor takes a long time to respond. "There's a part of me that wants to say no. There's a part of me that says 'you cannot abandon your people.' But it's said that to deny one's desires is to deny what makes one a goblin." Trevor looks up at you and smiles his delightful smile of fangs. "So yes, Gregory, yes! Let's leave this nightmare behind us and have an adventure!"

Which is exactly what you do.

**The End**

## Sixty

You reach out and grab the gnomish child by the back of his jumper.

"That's the spirit!" A'gog cheers.

You march the kid down the hall in front of you, holding him by his hair. He looks for all the world like a half-sized five-year-old. A'gog trails behind you, shouting directions at each intersection, and soon you find your way to a set of doors larger than any you've ever seen, flanked on either side by what you presume to be two five-year-old deep sea divers armed with crazy looking guns.

One of the guards aims a rifle at you, and you hold tighter onto your hostage, certain they will make an effective shield.

Unfortunately, your hostage is only as tall as your knee, and the guard aims for your face. A blinding beam of purple erupts against your skin, and you fall down. Your hostage turns on you, kicks you in the face, and soon you die under a flurry of blows.

### The End

### Sixty-One

"Oh, Gregory," Gu'dal says, beginning to cry. She takes the proffered ring and places it on her thumb, then crushes it with her fist so that it is small enough to stay on. "Thank you," she says. She leans over and licks your mouth with her raspy tongue, then looks you in the eye.

Tears well up in your eyes, and you return to your cot to sleep, happy, excited, and fearful. For the first time in your life, you've so much to lose. But also, so much to gain.

*Go to* **Sixty-Eight** *(page 104).*

## Sixty-Two

"If we start killing people, all we're going to do is scare the kabouters more, and drive them to look to Hak'kal for support," you say, and Sergei nods. A'gog doesn't look convinced, but concedes regardless.

You spend hours in that cramped ventilation tunnel, crafting phrases to emboss onto the walls of Underburg. It's frustrating work, because almost every idea you have, poetic and beautiful in English, sounds clichéd or dull in Kabouter. But eventually, you have your message.

That night—or the kabouters approximation of the same—, you emerge from hiding and set about your work. Actually, by and large, you and A'gog stand around and try to be silent while Sergei does all of the work.

You then make your way through the city—bumping into walls and occasionally people—and find your way to Sergei's apartment in the great hive.

"Now that we're inside, it's safe to talk," your host says.

"Could we possibly have a light?" you ask.

"Oh no," Sergei says, and you think it's possible that you've offended him.

"What do we do now?" A'gog asks.

"Sleep," Sergei suggests, "and in the morning I'll go out and see what there is to see."

You take him up on that, curling into a ball on the floor. You pull your jacket off to use as a pillow, and are asleep before you've much of a chance to think about how impossibly long your day has been.

You wake up some unknown number of hours later, still in the disconcerting dark. There is no sun outside this room, you realize, even if it were to have windows. You avoid letting your mind linger on such thoughts, because while trapped legions beneath the earth is a terrible time to invoke a bit of claustrophobia.

"Drink?" A'gog asks, pressing a glass into your hand.

You smell it—whisky?—and drink. "How'd you know I was awake?" you ask.

"You stopped snoring," A'gog replies.

"Oh."

"Our kabouter friend is off about his day, leaving us here to… to what? What is it we're hoping to accomplish anyhow? What is it that we, I mean you and I, can hope to do here?"

"I'm not sure," you say, "but we need to give the kabouters a chance to organize themselves. If they want to be free, but just need a little push, a little spirit, then it's worth being patient."

The day goes by slowly, and for an hour or so you agonize over trying not to go mad in the lonely dark. Then you realize that you're speaking with a goblin, and therefore are likely quite mad already, and time passes more smoothly.

"It will take more than one day to foment a revolution, it seems," Sergei says upon his return. "But with your help, tonight we'll plot new things to write upon the walls, new ways to inspire the revolt that lies dormant in the heart of every creature."

"You two can have fun with that. I'm not dying of old age while waiting for that spark. Because in my people, it's not dormant. It's alive. I'll wait there, if I'm to be waiting at all. Gregory? What are you going to do?"

*To stay around and see your plot through to its end, go to* **Seventy** *(page 106).*

*To give up on this whole adventure, state that you've had your fun but that it's time for you to return to your home on the surface, go to* **Seventy-Four** *(page 112).*

### Sixty-Three

A'gog, realizing you've made no move to grab the children, spurs his lion into motion, which chases down the slower of the two kids and mauls her.

"Are you serious?" you ask.

"I don't think you have the nerve for this sort of thing, sur-face-boy. We have lived as slaves our entire lives."

"Did that little kid enslave you?"

"Will killing her punish those who have killed so many of my people?"

"It isn't right," you say.

"You make a terrible libertine."

You turn your back on the lion-riding child-murdering goblin and leave the zoo behind. You half expect A'gog to ride you down, to die, to be devoured by a lion, but you're not so lucky.

Instead, you're captured by gnomes who enslave you and set you to spend the rest of your days breaking rocks and beating goblins. You die a decade later, miserable, broken, and sober.

### The End

### Sixty-Four

"Thank you," Trevor says, taking the ring in his small hand. He pulls a length of leather cord from one of the pockets on his vest and turns the ring into a pendant around his neck. He looks at you and smiles. You realize that he is as afraid of losing you as you are of losing him.

*Go to* **Sixty-Eight** *(page 104).*

## Sixty-Five

You tackle the kid on the right, put her in a headlock, and turn to A'gog. "What now?" you ask.

"Now we bring our hostage to the very gates of Hak'kal, make an appointment to see their ruling council, then let the lion eat them all."

"You're drunk," you say.

"So are you."

"Very well."

You hold your hostage in front of you and leave the zoo. A'gog, behind you, shouts out directions, and soon you find yourself in front of a menacing set of steel doors. They're larger than any you'd ever seen or imagined—although to be fair, you don't spend much of your time fantasizing about doors and the potential upper limits of their size—and are flanked by a pair of five-year-old boys in deep-sea-diver gear. With big crazy guns.

"Hey there," you say, as one points a rifle at you, "you boys go and get your parents cause I have a little kid and I'm not afraid to uh…"

"Kill her?" A'gog suggests.

"Well, actually I'm a bit afraid to kill her. I don't like the idea of killing a child, to be honest," you say back to A'gog.

"You have a councilgnome's daughter!" one of the guards says. "Release her at once!"

"I'd rather not?" you reply.

"What do you demand?" the guard asks.

"To uh, to see your leader." you say.

"Leaders. All of them," A'gog corrects.

"Yes. Yes, with the plurality. We demand the plurality be brought to us with all available haste!"

One guard keeps the rifle poised on you, while the other pulls a lever which opens the doors.

You try really hard to make sense of what lays beyond them, once you can see, but the sheer amount of sensory input overwhelms you and you lose what little ability to reason you had remaining. There are lights and crystals and clocks and gnomes and smiling happy children and there's opera and everything is blurry and...

And the lion is off at a sprint, tearing past the guards and into the city streets. A beam of purple light strikes you in the eyes, stinging and blinding, and you drop your hostage and wander aimlessly, drunkenly, into the city.

When your vision returns, you find yourself in an alley like any alley in the world above—except for the cavern roof two dozen feet above your head, of course. In front of you is a bank of levers that seem to run into a pipe. One of them is clearly labeled in sixteen different languages, including English: *do not pull.*

*To pull the lever, go to* **Sixty-Nine** *(page 105).*

*To refrain from pulling the lever, go to* **Seventy-Three** *(page 111).*

## Sixty-Six

"Just how drunk are you?" Yi'ta asks. "Do you think we haven't tried asking nicely? Do you think we spent generations enslaved without exploring all the different ways we could free ourselves?"

"All the same," you say, "I won't stand for this violence. Violence won't solve your problems, I promise you."

Yi'ta nods to Gu'dal, who unsheathes her blade and pulls it sharply across your thigh, causing you to collapse. As soon as you hit the ground, she stabs you in the throat.

As you lay bleeding—and strangely calm—the two goblins say something to one another in their own language and laugh. As you gurgle blood through your throat, they laugh all the harder. You'll never know what they said that was so funny, you realize. Then you die.

### The End

### Sixty-Seven

"Look, I won't sell you out to the council," you tell the gnome who stands beside you. It's clear that he doesn't understand your words. "I won't study you to them," you say, using his own phrasing. This he seems to understand. "But I *am* going to talk to them. The goblins appointed me to speak on their behalf, and I intend to do so."

"Bah," the man says, kicking your bed in anger. "You will talk, and they will talk. And talk talk talk talk talk talk talk…" He keeps saying the word "talk" as he climbs out the window and walks down the street. "Talk, talk, talk…"

You retire back to your bed and wake some unknown number of hours later. You suddenly understand why there are so many clocks in Hak'kal. They serve as some sort of replacement of the sun, for there is otherwise no easily distinguishable night or day.

*Go to* **Eighty** *(page 117).*

## Sixty-Eight

Pre-dawn finds you back in the gathering chamber, surrounded by hundreds, if not thousands of goblins. The approximate number of the little people is hard to gauge since they hang from ropes, cling to the ceiling, and generally refuse to stay still except when playing tiles or sleeping.

Gu'dal perches on the peak of a short stalagmite, clothed as she was the day you met her—a tailcoat and stovepipe hat. She fiddles with her cane, pulling the sword free and replacing it to pass the time.

Trevor stands beside you, decked in his full plate. He appears to be sleeping, vertical in his armor. He has a particularly frightening double-headed butcher knife held at his side.

For your own part, you've replaced your old cane with an unpretentious steel-headed one, complete with spike on the base. Not the sort of thing you'd have been caught dead carrying a half a year prior. You wear your bowler—because a gentleman must not abandon pride entirely—but you've got a breastplate made out of pewter dinner plates strapped to your chest and a pair of dark goggles that the goblins swear will protect your eyes from lightrifle blasts.

But appearances be damned, you're ready for war.

A stirring speech is made and stirs you, then the doors open. The horde takes off in a light jog through a massive tunnel, then pauses several hundred yards later for everyone to catch their breath.

As one, you run around the corner and into the first line of the gnomish defenses. The gnomes in front of you—for what else could the creatures be?—look like deep-sea divers in their copper helmets, and each bears the weapon you've been told is a lightrifle. They are nearly twice the size of a goblin, which is to say half the size of yourself, and they scream with what could be fear—or enthusiasm, as far as you would know—when you descend upon them.

You fight fiercely, using your height to your advantage and stepping over your foes to strike them from behind. Your cane shatters their faceplates, your spike finds their flesh.

The first line of defenses crumbles before the goblin horde, and you see the gates of their city lying shattered to your fore. Clearly, Yi'ta's machine in your clock tower above has served its purpose.

Suddenly, a lone riflegnome stands in the doorway and takes aim at you, the largest available target.

*To jump, go to* **Eighty-Three** *(page 123).*

*To duck, go to* **Eighty-Nine** *(page 128).*

*To dodge left, go to* **Ninety-One** *(page 130).*

*To dodge right, go to* **Ninety-Five** *(page 134).*


### Sixty-Nine

You never really liked to be told what to do, least of all by some half-pints with a big fancy city who seem to be enslaving most everyone they see. You reach out, cackle in a way you wouldn't were you sober, and pull the lever.

The wrong one, you realize. The "do not pull" lever is still up, but the one next to it, labeled *general alarm*, has been pulled.

Suddenly, green and yellow lights flash all about you, and six gnomish guards run towards you.

"Ah, hello there, fellows! How glad I am to see you!" you say, hoping to stall them long enough to think of something more clever to say.

They surround you, and you wish you could see their faces through the smoky glass of their helmets.

"I seem to have invaded your city while drunk," you say, trying to explain your situation. "You see, I drank some absinthe earlier this evening and swore allegiance of sorts to help your slaves revolt and utterly destroy you. Er… what I'm trying to get across is that I'm sorry?"

All six guards rush you, and though you try your hardest to swat them away and shush them as though they were rude children, they soon bring you to the ground. The last thing you see is a metal boot aimed towards your face.

**The End**

## Seventy

"You can't just expect people to throw away everything they've ever believed overnight," Sergei says.

"Yeah, I'm going to see this through, A'gog. If you want something done, you have to have patience."

"Sure, sure. Whatever. Goodbye. Good luck. Have fun." A'gog walks out the door after running into the wall in the dark—but only once.

And so begins your life in the dark city of Underburg. Each day, you ask Sergei the news, and each day it's the same. "Patience," he advises you.

You meet some of his friends, and after a few weeks, a gnome and a human from the city of Hak'kal move in to the apartment with you, agents of the gnomish Aboveground who arrive to help plot the grand revolution of the middle class. These two become your close friends as the weeks turn into months.

At some point, the months turn into a year, and you stop asking how the plot is going. You no longer even miss the light. You strike up an affair with the human, you eat the food that the Aboveground provides, and you write startling, epic poetry once you become fluent in Kabouter. Surely, you decide, if not this generation, than the next generation of kabouters will know your genius and will sing your praises. Or, you correct yourself, overthrow their gnomish masters.

It's not a bad life, in the dark city. Not a bad life at all.

## The End

### Seventy-One

Gu'dal grins at you, quite a disconcerting thing. With her bird-voice she says, "So you'll watch my back again, will you? I don't know what kind of good you'll do in a scrap with those bites on your leg, so what do you say we find you some guns and let you shoot anything that tries to kill us?"

A gun in your hand! You haven't held a gun since your brother left to head across the channel, taking both his poetic politics and his Colt revolver with him.

Outside the tower window, the first hints of twilight turn the skyline into something majestic. Hurried, Gu'dal leads you down the steps and out into the foggy morning. After several blocks, she turns the corner into a wide boulevard, lined at the side with the knickknack vendors you'd have called rag-and-bone men back home.

It's only after Gu'dal runs up and begins speaking to one quite hurriedly that you realize the shapes you'd mistook for ragged children are really a small army of goblins. Teeth and daggers flash in the first hint of sun. One human walks up to you and throws back his cowl, revealing the form of the old engineer you'd met the night before.

"Mr. Babbage?" you ask, surprised to see him among the combatants.

Instead of answering you, he hands you a pair of Remington revolvers. "Twelve shots," he says, then walks back to his stand.

Gu'dal runs back to stand in front of you, holding up a pocket watch for you to see. "One minute to go," she says, and you steel yourself.

Then, from somewhere, a bell tolls and the ground rises up like an ocean wave—sending fierce pain through your wounded legs—before crashing against the butcher shop across the street from you. You manage to keep your footing, but Gu'dal's top hat falls to the ground and she grimaces as she retrieves it.

For a long time, nothing out of the ordinary happens. Well, to be clear, nothing *new* that is out of the ordinary happens. You are still standing on a street, awake far before noon, with some four score goblins standing at arms besides you. What's more, you're beginning to sober up.

Then, after what could have been fifteen minutes or three hours, gnomes come pouring out of the doorways of the buildings across the street from you. Most wear bizarre copper and brass helmets that look adapted from undersea pressure suits and wield small rifles that shoot rays of purple and red and seem to inflict unbearable pain upon their targets. The boulevard becomes a warzone.

It doesn't take long for you to realize that you are vastly outmatched and outnumbered. Whatever the goblins expected, this wasn't it. Instead of rounding up stragglers, they face an organized assault.

Gu'dal, however, dives into the melee with a sadist's glee, dodging blows and rays as she draws her sword-cane across face after leg after neck. You stand resolutely behind her and fire your pistols. After nine shots, you've struck four gnomes and one goblin.

Then Gu'dal goes down under the blow of a lightrifle's butt. She shrieks like a wounded bird, but never rises again.

A gnome stands in front of you, face hidden behind armor, lightrifle aimed squarely at your chest.

*To surrender, dropping your remaining gun, go to* **Seventy-Nine** *(page 116).*

*To shoot the gnome and flee, go to* **Eighty-Four** *(page 123).*

*To shout, "Death to Hak'kal!" and continue to fight until your dying breath—which is presumably not so far from now—, go to* **Eighty-Six** *(page 125).*

### Seventy-Two

"Well I must say I've never been one to speak to monarchs on amiable terms," you say, "so perhaps it would be best if I were to accompany you and take up arms directly?"

"Slowly. English is my…" the gnome lifts up his fingers and begins to count. You suddenly realize that the gnomes have eleven digits: one hand has an extra opposable thumb on the far side of the pinky. "Seven… seventh. Seventh language."

You nod, and speak more slowly. "I will fight Hak'kal with you, for the goblin liberation."

"Good! It is good!" The gnome claps you on the thighs with both hands, in a gesture you take to be one of greeting. "My name is Comrade Eleven Stroke B."

"Gregory," you introduce yourself.

The door to your room swings open, and in comes an angry, drunken guard. She says something in Gnomish and swings at Eleven with the butt of her lightrifle.

Of pure instinct, you reach down and pick her up as though she were an impertinent child. She slams her helmeted head into the bridge of your nose, bloodying it, and you drop her.

"We go!" Eleven shouts, "Out the window!"

You do as ordered, clambering out the glassless window as quickly as possible, while Eleven kicks the fallen guard.

As soon as you are outside—or as "outside" as you're likely to get in this place!—Eleven dives headfirst through the window, landing in a practiced roll, clutching the guard's lightrifle across his chest.

He begins to run down the wide boulevard, and you follow. While it is easy to keep pace with his stride, you realize after four blocks that Comrade Eleven Stroke B. has far more endurance than you. Soon, too, you realize you've left your cane behind.

Ten breathless blocks later, he pulls you into an alley. Without giving you the opportunity to regain your wind, he leads you through a maze of side streets. The ceiling gets steadily lower, and you realize you must be nearing the city's edge. Finally, when the cavern roof becomes so low that you stoop, the gnome reaches up and pulls down a staircase from a trapdoor in the ceiling, as though it were a stairway into an attic. He leads you up.

*Go to* **Eighty-Two** *(page 120).*

## Seventy-Three

You stay your hand from disobeying for the sake of disobeying, and lean against the wall to think things through as best as your drunken state will allow.

And you lean right against the lever, pulling it down. A rumble and clank fills the air, and a piece of ceiling falls and clonks you soundly on the head, casting you into a comfortable blackness.

When you're roused, you see the sooty face of a human woman.

"Thank heavens, it was a dream. And what a marvelous dream!"

"What were you dreaming about," the woman asks, her accent Castilian.

"I was dreaming about..." you say, then sit up and take in your circumstances. "This. I was dreaming about this."

The woman laughs. "Well then, dreamer, my name is Comrade Difference Engine. And you are?"

"Gregory," you say, reasonably certain that you've gotten your name right.

"Comrade Gregory, you're a hero. You've saved us all."

"I did what?"

The woman from Spain explains everything to you. You released all of the pressure from the central boiler of Hak'kal—in order to pronounce the name of the city you're in you have to sound like you're about to spit, or like you're Dutch—and shut down most of the machinery of the city. The gnomes diverted power from the military generators, and the goblins attacked. Aided by the Aboveground of the city—which is what the resistance in an underground world is called—, the revolution was a resounding success and the whole empire is transitioning to a system that is half a workers' council and half a direct democracy.

"That sounds lovely," you say.

"It is," Comrade Difference Engine says.

"Care to kiss a hero?" you ask.

"No," Comrade Difference Engine replies.

"Alright then. Could you find me a drink?"

"That I can do," Comrade Difference Engine says, taking her leave of you.

"Sure am glad I pulled that lever," you say, then live out your life as the not-really-deserving folk hero of a egalitarian society full of mystery, wonder, steam engines, goblins, gnomes, kabouters, humans, and lions. You find meaningful physical work—designing and constructing elaborate and functional fountains—and while no one cares to hear your poetry, you are still very well regarded. You even drink less.

You never do find what became of A'gog, however.

**The End**

## Seventy-Four

"This one Guy Fawkes day," you tell your companions, "I went to a party that seemed quite promising. More absinthe and less baked potatoes, you understand. I let myself go a bit. I danced, I spoke at length with a startlingly attractive poet. I smoked and I watched the fires with joy. But at the end of the evening, there was nothing more to do. I hadn't succeeded in wooing, I hadn't delved any great new depths of consciousness. It was simply time to go home."

"What the hell are you talking about?" A'gog asks.

"My dear Sergei, I wish you the best of luck. A'gog? Call on me if you ever need my help: I dare say you'll know where to find me. But I think it's time for me to go home."

And so it goes. A'gog leads you back through the dark maze of corridors and crawlways, and soon you stand alone on the ground floor of your clock tower, the passageway under the stairs slamming behind you and inaccessible.

You make your way up your steps, open your door, and climb into your bed. You ignore the sunlight that streams in through your window and you sleep for a day.

You wake up with a headache worth dying over, and you never do ascertain if you'd been dreaming, hallucinating, or perfectly lucid. You never discover the fates of the slaves and their masters that bustle beneath your feet. But then, you'd never involved yourself with the bustle of the poor and the aristocracy outside your door, so perhaps this is no surprise.

Still, you've fodder for your poetry, though its strangeness is likely to condemn you to obscurity. But if such is to be your fate, you will meet it head on with the civility and drunkenness that you bring to all your endeavors.

**The End**

### Seventy-Five

Twenty minutes later you are at the fairgrounds accompanied by a nervous Gu'dal. You've a beautiful (but sadly muzzle-loaded and antique) rifle strapped across your back, a spyglass in a leather satchel on your side.

"I stole this idea from Nadar, a man of my brother's acquaintance. He organized a fleet of balloons to aid in the defense of the Paris Commune. Quite a fellow. Famous photographer, too. Took my brother's portrait." You explain this to Gu'dal, your voice filling a bit with pride when you think of your exiled and imprisoned elder brother. Your goblin companion, however, doesn't appear to understand you in the least.

Unfortunately for you, an elderly fellow is currently attending to the balloon you hoped to commandeer. He's stoking the fire in the brazier, most likely preparing to launch at sunrise to draw attention to the fair. He is, however, the only person in sight.

"We need that balloon?" Gu'dal asks.

"Yeah," you reply.

Gu'dal draws her sword from her cane and smiles.

*To calm Gu'dal down, then attempt to beguile the attendant, plying him with spirits, go to* **Eighty-Eight** *(page 126).*

*To allow Gu'dal to handle the attendant in her fashion, go to* **Ninety-Three** *(page 133).*

## Seventy-Six

"We'll be out here," you whisper. "Inside, we'd just slow you down."

"Alright," Sergei says. "Wish me luck."

You nod, though of course, Sergei doesn't hear you.

You pass the next five minutes wondering whether Sergei can see at all without screeching. If he's trying to be silent will he even know where he is? You decide that he can probably echolocate based on the noises about him, but just as you begin down this next train of thought, you hear a blood-curdling screech—even more piercing than the usual—and footsteps running towards you from inside the building.

A'gog has the torch lit in seconds, and you are stunned by the city around you.

*To stare at Underburg, a place you're not likely to see again and who's details you'd love to express in poetry one day, go to* **Eighty-Five** *(page 124).*

*To pull your cane and pay attention to the fight that seems to be heading your way, go to* **Ninety** *(page 129).*

### Seventy-Seven

"Look you, I don't know the whole of your difficulties with the gnomish establishment, but I do know that the gnomes have treated me with civility and grace! I plan on speaking with them, not running around on some madcap adventure!" You speak rapidly in your anger, and it is clear that your would-be revolutionary rescuer understands only your tone.

"Guards! Guards!" you shout.

The handsome gnome throws himself headfirst through the window opening, landing nimbly on the ground outside in a roll.

Not three seconds later, a guard open the door to your room, clearly drunk. "Yes? Yes? You have been yelling. Have you had poor dreams?" she says, walking towards you, her lightrifle hanging loosely at her side.

*To attack the guard, capture her rifle, and follow your rescuer with intent to apologize, go to* **Eighty-Seven** *(page 125).*

*To report the interloper to the guard, go to* **Eighty-One** *(page 120).*

## Seventy-Eight

You slip cautiously into the building, feeling with your hands. Fortunately, the ceiling is a hair's breadth above your head, and as long as you walk carefully, you don't need to crouch.

You make your way perhaps a hundred yards before a question occurs to you: "Can you see without screeching? Since we're trying to be quiet, I mean, I wonder how you know where you're going?"

"Shut up!" Sergei whispers, but it's too late.

Words in Kabouter are shouted from quite nearby.

"They asked who we were," A'gog translates.

"Oh," you say.

*To attempt to beguile the guards or officers or whoever it is that is hailing you, go to* **Ninety-Two** *(page 131).*

*To answer reasonably honestly (perhaps excluding the bit about poison) and appeal to their humanity, go to* **Ninety-Four** *(page 133).*

## Seventy-Nine

You let the revolver slip from your fingers and hit the pavement. Owing to your hyper-focus, it rings out loudly, clearly over the din of battle as it strikes the ground. You raise your hands above your head.

The gnome shoots you regardless, and everything goes black.

When you come to, you find yourself naked in a human-sized birdcage swinging in near-total darkness. Far beneath you, you see the lights of a strange city that must be Hak'kal. It's beautiful, in its way.

On the floor of the cage is a small bowl filled with something that smells like oatmeal. Next to it is a sign, written in sixteen different languages. In English, it says: "Sing, and you eat. The louder and more beautifully you sing, the better you eat."

And thus do you spend the rest of your days, a caged bird. You may sing or not. In the end, it truly makes no difference, because you will never again see the stars, never again hold a conversation. Never again will you wander the streets drunk and unruly, never again will feel the touch of another. The difference between life and death is so thin as to be transparent.

## The End

## Eighty

A guard—a different one from the night before, you are nearly certain—takes you from your cell and walks you through the city streets. This time, you've only one armed gnome accompanying you. Clearly, by not escaping the night before through your open window, you have proven that you are either amiable or know that you have nowhere to go.

The streets are full of laughter and pleasantries, with every gnome of every gender doffing his or her cap to every passerby, including your silent guard and yourself. A cooper makes a barrel from metal staves, her cheeks a ruddy complexion, a smile on her face and a tune on her lips.

Everyone, and everything, is downright jolly. Except for yourself. You're not certain you've *ever* been jolly in your adult life—at least not while sober—and certainly, it is disconcerting to be surrounded by so many happy, smiling, slave-keeping creatures.

You're led, in short order, up and into a building carved out of a momentous stalagmite that reaches up, connects to its corresponding stalactite, and disappears into the darkness above.

After witnessing the massive clockworks, crystals, mirrors, and general technological madness outside, the inside of the building seems rather austere. The ground floor—as you have no choice, it seems, but to refer to this room so far beneath the earth—is a single massive room, a circle of some one hundred paces in diameter. The ceiling is twice your height above you. Three flaming braziers light the place, and the walls are plain and featureless.

An empty throne sits in the center of the room, and a semi-circle of smaller chairs surrounds it. In these sit two-dozen gnomes, speaking quite animatedly in Gnomish. Most are dressed like any other gnome you've seen on the streets outside, in plain work clothes or casual attire, although quite conspicuous is a young gnome child in a one-piece jumper and an older fellow decked to the nine hells in gold and jewels.

Your guard walks you into the center of their semi-circle, signaling for you to stand in front of the throne. She then turns, pulls off her helmet, and tugs at her ears in a comic and exaggerated way that you decide must be some sort of gnomish salute. She replaces her helmet and walks out the building, leaving you to the council.

"Please, have a seat," a very elderly gnome says in excellent English—with a bit of a French accent.

You look at the throne. "Here?" you ask.

"Of course."

And so you sit in the throne, surrounded by what you presume to be the government of Hak'kal. The child laughs and whispers something into a neighbor's ear. You are quite certain that the child is laughing at you.

"I'm here to speak on behalf of the goblins," you say, because it's the truth. "I want to negotiate peace."

When you speak, one of the gnomes in work clothes translates your words into Gnomish. By watching their reactions, you realize that only three or four of the councilgnomes speaks English. You hope that your interpreter is a good one.

"Of course," the elderly gnome says. "We want peace very badly. We, the council, have ourselves been tasked with helping the goblins. A representative that they trust would be a welcome ally."

You have absolutely no idea if you believe the gnome, you realize. You have absolutely no idea what to believe at all. You dearly miss your drugs. Wormwood never lies to you. Well, except when it does.

"I'd like you to take a tour of Hak'kal. I think it's important." The gnome speaks in a voice that betrays that his request is not actually a request. "Anywhere you'd like to go."

"Take him to the schools!" the child says. "The schools are wonderful!" This is, you decide, quite an unnatural and unnerving thing for a child to say.

"The engineering district," grumbles a middle-aged councilgnome in a canvas smock and heavy boots—where do they get the fibers for canvas?

"I don't know," you say. "It doesn't matter so much to me. Truthfully I'd just like a drink. Perhaps brandy?"

But the councilgnomes seem to ignore your request for refreshment, and the interpreter doesn't bother interpreting.

"Alright," you say, "I'll take a tour."

*To visit the school district, go to* **Ninety-Seven** *(page 137).*

*To visit the engineering district, go to* **One Hundred** *(page 142).*

## Eighty-One

"If it was a dream, it was a dream with rather terrible manners," you say, then report to the guard about the interloper, your would-be rescuer.

The guard nods. "I'll take that into advisement. I would suggest however," she says, "that you not tell any others that you've had involvement with the Aboveground. The council will not take it well."

"But I had no involvement! I reported to you as soon as I saw one of them!" you protest.

"Look, just listen to me. It won't win you any favors. Forget about the Aboveground. If you see one of them again, say nothing of it to anyone. Good night."

You don't understand the guards agitation, but she walks out of the door without explaining herself to any real degree. You lay back on the bed, and sleep overcomes you before you manage to worry yourself overmuch further.

You wake up what feels to be the next day—for there is no sun with which to tell time, nor is your watch in working order—and rub the sleep out of your eyes. Sure enough, you're still in an easily escapable cell in an inescapable city some unknown depth under the city you had presumed to call home.

*Go to* **Eighty** *(page 117).*

## Eighty-Two

You are momentarily blinded by the brightness of the room above the city street. Even after your eyes have adjusted, the great cacophony—both auditory and visual—keeps you from processing what you see.

A good half-minute later, you finally wrap your sleepless brain around your surroundings: you stand in a room the size of a small café with a ceiling no more than a hand's breadth higher than your head. A great many machines are clattering and clanging and a great many people are attending to them. A dozen gnomes pack envelopes into pneumatic canisters that are whisked away by two score pneumatic tubes. Half a dozen goblins ride miniature, stationary penny-farthings, powering a great leather-and-copper bellows. A human woman turns knobs and pulls levers on a mysterious and massively complex machine. Four creatures that you don't recognize—of stature similar to the gnome's, pasty-pale with gigantic unseeing eyes—are calculating with over-sized brass abaci and yelling numbers in Spanish to the human.

Above the din of work rises the din of laughter and play, for it is clear that everyone is enjoying her or himself. Blazing gas lamps light the place, leaving no trace of deep shadow.

For your part, you have just been standing there, mouth slightly agape, stomach churning in the aftermath of adrenaline and exertion.

After a moment, one of the letter-writing gnomes takes notice of your presence and walks over to converse with Eleven Stroke B. in Gnomish. The gnome is wearing the near-ubiquitous coveralls—with various glass vials of ink held by loops across her breast—and has feathery pen quills protruding from her hat at jaunty and ill-considered angles.

After hearing from Eleven, she turns to you and speaks in accented but fluent English: "Welcome, Comrade Gregory. You have come to put yourself in the service of the Aboveground, to seek liberty and freedom?"

You nod.

"Your face, it's bloody. Please, let me lead you to the washroom. After that, you may sleep. In the morning, I or someone else will answer all of your questions." Your new guide takes you behind the gigantic bellows, into a hallway—need it even be said that this hallway is lined with pipe and apparatus?—, and into a small shower room.

There are faucets set into the wall, showerheads in the ceiling, and drains in the floor. Mirrors line the room at knee and waist level—for goblins, gnomes, and those other creatures, you assume—and a single small mirror is placed at approximately your own eye level.

You are, in case you were curious, a complete mess. Your bowler is dented, your jacket covered with dust, and your face quite bloodied. You need a shave and a shower. But more than that, you need sleep. You wash the blood off your face with soap and water.

"What's your name," you ask your guide.

"You may call me Comrade Pneumatic H. Fourteen."

"Are all of you gnomes named with numbers?" you ask.

"No, no. When we join the Aboveground, it's customary to take on a new name. Usually, after a machine dear to our hearts. A Pneumatic H. Fourteen is a type of air-compressor used in the message delivery system. It's a bit outdated, but it's what I learned on."

"And Eleven Stroke B.?"

"It's a type of light-cannon. It was developed to penetrate faceshields and permanently blind."

"Interesting," you say, as Pneumatic H. Fourteen leads you into a tiny room with a bunk bed. Neither of the bunks is occupied.

*To take the top bunk, go to* **One Hundred and Two** *(page 145).*

*To take the bottom bunk, go to* **Ninety-Eight** *(page 139).*

## Eighty-Three

You leap into the air, and the purple beam of light catches you in the leg. A pain worse than fire—well, you've never really been burned, but you can suppose—shoots up into your chest, and you collapse to the ground, bashing your head on the stone. Your mind goes a bit fuzzy, you long for a sip of absinthe, and you die.

**The End**

## Eighty-Four

You raise your weapon to fire, and both of you shoot simultaneously. Fortunately, the leaden bullet has immediate effect upon the chest of the gnome, while the purple ray has only enough time to hurt you immensely. Your foe drops the raygun and collapses into the street while you limp away unsteadily, having lost your cane.

Although a few more beams scatter about you, you make good your slow escape and stumble until the sounds of battle are far behind you.

Once you're back into a familiar neighborhood of vice and low culture, you sell your revolvers and stumble into an opium den. Opium, you think. That's good for what ails you. Soon enough, it will all be forgotten. Perhaps you'll even write a book about your adventures. A fantasy, of course you'll have to call it. And perhaps that's what it all was.

The sweet, floral taste of opium smoke goes through your mouth and into your lungs, and soon you recline on the couch to sleep.

**The End**

## Eighty-Five

The city is the most beautiful and alien thing you've ever seen. Every surface but the floor glistens, every wall is clearly hand-shaped with love and care. It looks a bit like pictures of the Casbah, in that the buildings seems stacked atop one another and are formed by an organic logic that isn't immediately visible. Just as it occurs to you that the walls themselves are built so as to reflect sound in useful—or perhaps just aesthetically pleasing—ways, you see two kabouters come running from an alley across the way, brandishing knives and looking like quite unpleasant people all around.

You turn when you hear Sergei shout "Success!" as he runs out of the building, chased by two additional guards. A'gog has taken one of them by the leg with his teeth while Sergei holds a second at bay with his fists. No more seem to be coming from within the building, so you turn to face the two newcomers.

You remind yourself that they're half your height, and strike one down with a lucky blow from your cane as soon as he or she or it or whatever is within range.

The other darts past your reach and stabs you in the thigh. You drop your cane in shock, pick up the miserable little creature, and throw it with your enraged might into the side of the building.

You pant, exhausted, and examine the scene once more. All four guards lie facedown, dead. So does A'gog.

"We've got to go," Sergei says.

You grab A'gog's body, the torch flickers out against the cold stone floor, Sergei grabs your arm, and you run for it.

*Go to* **One Hundred and One** *(page 143).*

### Eighty-Six

The world seems to go silent as you cock the hammer and pull the trigger. You don't hear the report of the powder igniting, nor the crack of the glass of the gnome's helmet. Nor do you hear a scream. But who could die without a scream?

Several blood-drenched minutes later, you learn the answer. *You* could die without a scream. In fact, you do. You die in the arms of your goblin comrades, having given yourself fully to the cause of their freedom. But regardless, you still die.

### The End

### Eighty-Seven

"I saw a spider," you say to the guard, "up there, on the wall." You point to a spot behind the guard.

"Where?" the guard asks, turning her back to you. You snatch the lightrifle away and attempt to knock her unconscious with the butt of it. This, however, perhaps owing to her helmet—or perhaps owing to your general inexperience in the art of violent conflict—proves unsuccessful.

"Give me back my lightrifle," the gnome insists, jumping up towards the gun, which you hold above your head and well out of her reach.

You give your captor a good, solid kick—well executed, it must be said!—, grab your hat, coat, and cane, and dive out the window headfirst. However, unlike the acrobatic young gnome who did likewise before you, you are unable to perform the requisite roll, and thusly your nose is bloodied. Your cane skitters away from you.

You stand up and see the representative from the gnomish Aboveground fleeing down an unlit street, and run, exhausted, to catch up. You leave your cane behind.

"Why did you say for the guards?" your rescuer asks when you finally close the gap between the two of you.

"I uh," you begin, "I thought it would be a good opportunity to commandeer a weapon." You hand the lightrifle to the gnome.

"Good thought!" the gnome says. "Call me Comrade Eleven Stroke B."

"Gregory," you introduce yourself.

Comrade Eleven Stroke B. leaves the boulevard and leads you through a maze of alleys. The ceiling gets steadily lower, and you realize you must be near the city's edge. Finally, when the cavern roof becomes so low that you stoop, the gnome reaches up and pulls down a staircase from a trapdoor in the ceiling, as though it were a stairway into an attic. He leads you up.

*Go to* **Eighty-Two** *(page 120).*

## Eighty-Eight

"I think I can handle this without any bloodshed," you say to your companion, "but you'll need to stay back here in the shadows."

"I suppose. But we don't have much time. And besides," she says, "he's only an old hu–"

You look at her in horror and she realizes what she almost said. "My apologies," she says. "The gnomes talk about humans like you're simply livestock. I forget sometimes to ignore what they've raised me to believe." With that, she puts away her sword. You hand her the rifle, which she holds like a pike since it is three times her height.

"Good morning!" you announce to the caretaker as you walk up, concealing your limp as best as you can.

The man looks surprised to see you.

"Have a drink with me, boss?" You ask, offering a flask of brandy from under your vest.

"I'm... I'm sorry?" The gentleman asks, clearly far from fluent in English. You mentally curse yourself for forgetting the language barrier.

Your plan was to convince him that you were a new hire, quite familiar with a balloons, then abscond with the lighter-than-air craft once he passed out drunk. But you had forgotten that you don't speak enough French to do more than order drinks and flirt.

"Gu'dal," you say, "I believe your plan will have its purpose after all."

The man looks even more confused, as you addressed this last bit as though you were still talking to him.

You take a sip of your brandy, and try to look relaxed.

Suddenly, a swift goblin comes sprinting down the path, sword in one hand and cane in the other, top hat somehow staying put upon her head.

The caretaker turns his back to you and you take the opportunity to strike him on the back of the head with your cane, hoping to knock him out.

"*Jésus-Christ! Tu m'as frappé à l'arrière de la tête avec une canne, vous trou du cul!*" he says, turning back to you.

Gu'dal drops her sword, takes a running jump, and lands on his back. She pulls her cane up along one side of his throat and compresses. Four short seconds later, he collapses unconscious on the ground.

"Get the balloon in the air. We have only seconds. And give me your brandy," Gu'dal commands.

You pass Gu'dal the flask and run to retrieve your rifle. Then you climb aboard the wicker gondola, piling more wet straw and oiled fabric onto the brazier. Soon, the balloon begins to rise. Gu'dal splashes brandy on the caretaker's collar, drops the flask by his hand, retrieves her sword, and hops aboard.

As you lift into the air, she tells you, "You know you can't actually just hit someone on the back of the head to knock them out, right? I mean, you're as likely to kill them as knock them out."

"Of course," you bluff, "I was just trying to distract him. But, uh, what was it that you did?"

"Sleep hold. You stop blood from reaching the brain without blocking the airway. It puts them down, but not for very long."

"Ah," you say.

"Now, you know how to control this thing?"

"Control?"

*Go to* **Ninety-Six** *(page 134).*


### Eighty-Nine

You duck, but while crouching you are an easier target still, and the purple beam of light catches you in the face. Perhaps the goggles have saved your eyes, but it is the rest of your head that burns with pain, forcing you to collapse. A lanky form shoots forward from the horde and brings down your assailant with a well-struck sword-blow, but you are wounded too seriously to continue.

A goblin horde does not bother with combat medics, it seems, because you are left where you lie, and the horde storms around you and into the city of Hak'kal. They might have won, too. But you don't know, because you die slowly, fading in and out of painful consciousness for what might be hours or merely seconds. Eventually, you drift away forever.

**The End**

## Ninety

You steel your nerve and lift your cane. Actually, you decide, perhaps you merely copper your nerves, because even in this moment before a fight, that lovely drug adrenaline pumping through you, you do *not* feel as though you have nerves of steel. Certainly more copperish. Which is prettier anyhow, you realize, and certainly strong enough for cookware.

Sergei runs out door at an incredible speed, and you stick your foot into the doorway after he's through, tripping the guard who follows. You see A'gog with his teeth latched on to the second pursuer's leg, and things are looking good.

Until you feel the warm, wet feeling of a blade run down your backside. You collapse, uncertain of who has laid you low, and die.

**The End**

## Ninety-One

You dodge to the left and the purple beam passes harmlessly beside you before diffracting on the wall. Before you can blink, and certainly before you can recover your wits, Gu'dal has crossed the gulf between the horde and your assailant and has cut his chest open so that his child-sized guts pour out, hot onto the stone.

You rush after her, and the horde follows with you. You storm through the city gates and witness Hak'kal, an underground metropolis of majestic stonework and fanciful clocks.

It's through this city that you dash, drunk on adrenaline—and booze, of course—, fighting the few guards who attempt to delay you. Most of the gnomes, non-combatants, surrender and are escorted to a building that serves as a jail. Some gnomes—and humans, and strange, giant-eared creatures you learn to call kabouters—join you in your fight and are welcomed in your ranks.

When at last you reach the halls of government, the city guard puts up a fight. At the front lines, you are standing next to Gu'dal when she falls, the butt of a lightrifle crushing her skull. The spike of your cane finds her killer's chest, and you lift his lifeless body over your head and dash it against the council building.

The fight is soon over, and you sit down to weep. You are alive, still, and miraculously unharmed, but so many lie dead about you. So many goblins, so many gnomes.

"Thank you," Trevor says to you, "thank you."

You look down at him—for even when you are sitting, his head is below your own—with red eyes. His meet yours through the facemask of his helmet, and the two of you begin to sob together.

There is no cheering upon the victory, something you find odd but that Trevor explains: "the fight is when we celebrate. The victory? The victory is a beginning that is marked by loss. We mourn our dead and theirs, we mourn the long years that we lost to slavery."

"When will you celebrate, then?" you ask.

"When we next have something to fight," Trevor says, pulling off his helmet. A smile cracks, complete with black gums and razor teeth. "And, of course, when next we drink!"

For a moment, you manage to smile yourself. You think that you will stay here, in the undercity. Smallish they may be, you feel like you have found your people.

### The End

### Ninety-Two

"Envoy from Hak'kal," you say.

"What? What is an envoy?" a voice asks in very simple and heavily accented English.

"I was sent from Hak'kal to talk to you about the goblin situation."

"What goblin situation?"

While you're talking, Sergei takes his hand from your elbow and disappears silently into the dark.

"The goblins are up to something," you say.

"The goblins are always up to something," the voice responds.

You continue in this way for the better part of ten minutes, confusing the officers and occasionally tossing in words that you are certain they will not know.

"It's very important that I beguile you," you say to the officers.

"What is beguile? Why have they sent you if you do not speak Kabouter?" the officer asks.

"Because they understand how important it is to me to find a terminal solution to the continued impediment that is presented by your existence," you say.

"I don't understand you at all! Guards!" But those are the last words the officer ever speaks, because soon the room is filled with the sound of retching and a strange feeling of death that you're not sure how you've identified.

"They're all dead," Sergei announces, after screeching once.

"Ah, hell, so am I," A'gog announces.

You whirl in the darkness but see nothing. You hear a body—A'gog's, you presume—fall to the floor, and two screeches sound from two different people. You hear a tussle, and the sound of a knife repeatedly entering a body, and nearly lose control of your bowels owing to your fright.

"Let's get out of here," Sergei says, and takes your arm. You run. Once you're back outside, Sergei hands you A'gog's body. "He died in service to his people and mine," Sergei says, as though words could comfort you.

You realize with horror that you're not actually saddened by A'gog's death. You're just, well, startled and confused. And very, very overwhelmed.

*Go to* **One Hundred and One** *(page 143).*

### Ninety-Three

Gu'dal runs charging ahead of you, straight towards the old caretaker. She raises her blade up above her head, holding it two-handed. As she nears him, he turns to see her, a look of horror on his wrinkled face. She jumps vertically something like three times her own height, bringing her head level with his, then draws her blade across his throat swiftly, ending his life.

For a moment, you're paralyzed with awe and fear. Then you drain your flask of brandy and drop it on the ground. Then, and only then, you approach Gu'dal. "You know, you didn't need to kill him."

"Oh," Gu'dal says, "I suppose…" she thinks for a moment. "I suppose that wasn't the most ethical thing to do."

You look at each other awkwardly, then resume the dead man's work of preparing the balloon for takeoff. Gu'dal climbs into the wicker basket beside you and hands you wet straw to throw into the brazier. Soon, the lighter-than-air craft takes off.

*Go to* **Ninety-Six** *(page 134).*

### Ninety-Four

"My name is Gregory," you say, "and I'm from the city above. I've come to talk things out."

If A'gog is giving you a piercing stare, one that would shoot horror into your veins and turn you to ice, you don't notice because it's pitch black.

"Speak slowly," a voice says in very heavily accented English.

"I want to talk about the situation with Hak'kal," you say, "because I'm concerned with how the gnomes are treating you."

"Sit down," the voice says, and you comply.

"The disturbance the other day. Is that you?"

"I didn't mean to cause you trouble," you say.

Suddenly, you hear Sergei screech to your left, and cold arms are pinning you to the floor.

*To struggle against them, go to* **Ninety-Nine** *(page 141).*

*To tell A'gog to light the torch, that it's your only hope, go to* **One Hundred and Three** *(page 147).*

### Ninety-Five

You dodge to your right, and the purple beam catches you right in the chest. The pain drives you into anger, and you charge forward, your cane overhead. But you never reach your assailant. The lightrifle beam lays you low. You feel no pain, however. You have adrenaline to thank for that.

In fact, you feel nothing, ever again.

### The End

### Ninety-Six

"So basically, we throw more straw on the fire to go higher," you explain to Gu'dal, "and let it burn down to go lower. To move around, we find the altitude with the proper wind. Then when we get where we're going, we drop a rope and your friends tie us to the ground."

"That's insane," the goblin replies. "You're trusting entirely to chaos."

You grin.

Luck is with you, because as the sun appears over the horizon you find yourself spitting distance—literally, as you test—from an assembled mess of goblins on the ground disguised as street children. You drop the rope and are soon anchored to a rag-and-bone-man's cart of knickknacks.

You load your rifle, overseen by Gu'dal, then pull out the spyglass and search the streets below.

"I wish I was on the ground. Or better," Gu'dal says, "below it. I wasn't meant to be up here in the air."

"You'll be fine."

"I know I'll be fine. I'm just not happy."

As you bicker, a rumble breaks the early morning calm, and the ground below shakes, knocking goblins to their feet. A shockwave ripples up your tether, bouncing the basket about most uncomfortably. Gu'dal's face goes from its usual healthy green to a strange pale.

"Give me the rifle," she says, piling up the loose straw into a mound so that she can see over the edge. "I'm a better shot than you."

Not accustomed to killing, you do so. And moments later, the streets below turn into a warzone.

Armed and armored gnomes come pouring out of the doorways to buildings, but they don't look like fearful refugees. They look like a coordinated strike force. They wield frightening lightrifles that shoot purple and red beams that seem to cause insufferable pain in their victims and they fight with a calm intensity you've never before imagined.

Gu'dal fires shot after shot while you look on with horror. It is clear that the goblin forces are being slaughtered. Not five minutes after it began, it is over. The gnomes are triumphant and the goblins lie dead.

Gu'dal looks at the tether, and you realize she is planning on descending to the streets below.

*To allow her to climb down towards the gnomes—and near-certain death—go to* **One Hundred and Four** *(page 148).*

*To take her blade and cut the tether, saving her from such a suicidal act, go to* **One Hundred and Eight** *(page 153).*

*To allow the balloon to descend where it is and join her in a final stand against the merciless gnomes, go to* **One Hundred and Twelve** *(page 157).*

### Ninety-Seven

The child—whose name turns out to be Germinal—bounces his way through the streets, waving at colleagues and running up behind friends to cover their eyes and demand that they "guess who."

But despite these distractions, you find yourself in short order at perhaps the most bizarre school you've ever seen. In the classroom, gray-bearded gnomes of all genders sit studiously and are taught by adolescents!

You tell Germinal that, where you are from, the children are taught by adults.

"Well, that's absurd," your guide points out. "Children learn things quite naturally in the course of work and life. It's the old gnomes who get all curmudgeonly, who need an extra nudge to learn new things, to understand the times. Maybe it's different in the sunlight?"

"Maybe," you respond, and file the idea away as something to consider later. For the moment, you're caught up in the lesson plan.

"You see, goblins are every bit as sentient as gnomes," the teacher explains. "They experience pain, and emotion, at *least* as sharply as we do."

"What do you mean, *at least?*" one of the students asks.

"Well, goblins are very smart. Nearly as smart as ourselves. *Nearly.* But the goblin is more in touch with their animal brain than a gnome is. It's all very noble—it allows them a closer connection to their spirits, their hearts. In many ways, the goblins, dumb as they are, have a leg up on us!"

The adults in the room nod with comprehension, and you step outside to sip liquor from the flask you keep in your left coat pocket. When it's drained, you begin to sip from the flask in your right coat pocket. You're suddenly overcome with emotion. What emotion, you're not certain.

Germinal leaves the school building and joins you sitting on the steps. After letting you ponder for a moment longer, he starts talking. "You must think us monsters, us gnomes. I'm sure the goblins told you about the conditions they live in."

You nod.

"Goblins shouldn't be treated like animals. Even the conservative thinkers of my generation know they deserve to be treated as well as the kabouters."

"Kabouters?" you ask.

"Yes, the kabouters. They're uh… they're another species, like the goblins or the humans."

"Are they your slaves too?" The liquor has loosened your tongue, as is its way.

"No, they're not. They're here because we help them, and they help us. They do a lot of the maintenance in the outlying tunnels. They couldn't feed themselves without us, and we couldn't, you know, process the stuff that they process."

"Stuff?"

"Yeah. They like, deal with our, uh… our sewage."

"Interesting," you say. "So the goblins should be treated as well as your well-treated servants?"

"Of course!"

It occurs to you that, perhaps, children—or at least Germinal—aren't good at picking up sarcasm.

"But then there are the radicals among us, too. The radicals want the goblins freed completely, given back some of the deeper tunnels. The radicals think that goblins, given free will, would mine even more efficiently, that we could trade essentials for the ore that they mine."

"Hrmm," you say. You decide to keep your opinions about the self-serving "good will" of these radicals to yourself. "And where do you stand?"

"Where do I stand? I stand nowhere. I'm a politician, after all!"

"Of course. Of course." You drain the last of the second flask and rise to your unsteady feet. Thanks to the magic of alcohol, you can feel every slight tremor that runs through the floor.

"Back to the council?" Germinal asks.

And off you go.

*Go to* **One Hundred and Five** *(page 149).*

## Ninety-Eight

You throw yourself onto the bottom bunk and fall asleep before you have time to remove your hat or mumble your thanks. Your dreams are simple and pleasant, of your friends and lovers in the above world, of walks along the canals, of foods finer than you can afford.

Some unknown number of hours later, you awaken refreshed. You pull the bowler off from over your eyes and see that your room has had its lantern lit. You sit up in bed and see the human woman from the previous night sitting on the floor, tugging thick brown boots on over the legs of her coveralls. Her hair is short and black, her skin a light olive, and now that you can see her close up, you realize that she is most likely five or more years your senior.

"Morning," she says, her voice pleasant enough, though tired, her accent clearly Castilian.

"Good morning," you say.

"Didn't get a chance to meet you when you came in last night, face all a-bloody. Name's Comrade Difference Engine."

"Gregory," you say, shaking her proffered hand.

"When'd you come underground?" she asks.

"Last night."

"You from the city up there?"

"Indeed. Are you not?"

"No. Born in España, was living in England when those bastard gnomes got me, dragged me under."

"They kidnap humans?" you ask, surprised.

"Sometimes. Singers and engineers, mostly."

"Which are you, then?"

"Know what a Difference Engine is?" she asks.

"No."

"It's a mechanical calculator. My professor at Cambridge," Difference waits for you to look suitably impressed, which you do, "designed it. I was working late one night with Mr. Babbage in his office when the gnomes raided the place and stole the plans and, well, myself. They stole me off in some kind of aquatic, sub-marine vehicle. Haven't seen daylight since.

Happy as damnation that the Aboveground took it upon themselves to rescue me. What about yourself?"

"Well I uh…" you recognize that your story pales in comparison, "I'm a writer, by trade. Between employments, as it were. And a right mess of goblins took it upon themselves to occupy my clock tower…" You tell your brief tale while Comrade Difference Engine leads you out of your room, through the hallway and into a large cafeteria.

The cafeteria is filled with almost two score of the smaller people, mostly gnomes, all gabbing and laughing. Your guide beelines for the back of the room, where she fills a ceramic mug with coffee from an overly-complex boiler. She blows on it, smells it, and smiles.

"Can't live without the stuff."

*Go to* **One Hundred and Nine** *(page 154).*

## Ninety-Nine

You throw your captor off of you easily, knowing her or him or it to weigh half of what you do. But where two hands were, there are now eight, and you struggle in vain. You're forced to the floor and the life is choked out of you in the dark, leagues away from the surface, from your few friends, from the comfort of letters and vice. Unseeing and unseen, you die.

## The End

## One Hundred

The councilgnome in the canvas smock—whose name turns out to be Emile—marches you through the maze-like streets of Hak'kal, occasionally stopping to curtsy to passersby. He seems gruff, though likably gruff, and he says little as you find yourself in a denser and denser mess of crystals, clockwork, and steam.

What's more, you begin to see goblins at work, side-by-side with gnomes.

"I wanted to show you this," Emile says, "because I wanted you to know that there are goblins who live good lives. They work on real, meaningful tasks, because they are smart enough to."

But you pick up on something. Most of the goblins you see are smiling, but not every smile is genuine. You've always had a knack for reading people—except at cards, most unfortunately!—and the goblins here have sadness behind their eyes, you're sure of it.

Your guide continues: "The goblins have come to see us as siblings, not masters. You might resent your older brother sometimes, yes, but you know that what he's doing, he's doing with your best interests at heart. The goblins, before we came, lived like animals. Now, they help engineer the greatest city the world has ever seen!"

Pride cracks through the curmudgeonly gnome's rough exterior, and you realize he believes what he's saying with the earnestness of a true believer. He believes it as truly as you believe in vice.

But suddenly, out of the corner of your eye, you see a goblin with a wrench who is about to turn violent. She must have overheard Emile's speech, and she must have disagreed. She bounds up onto a gnome-height gear that stands before her, turns, and prepares to leap and attack your host.

*To throw Emile out of harm's way, go to* **One Hundred and Seven** *(page 152).*

*To step back and observe, go to* **One Hundred and Ten** *(page 156).*

## One Hundred and One

You reach the ventilation tunnel undisturbed and set A'gog down.

"Can I light the torch here?" you ask.

"Let's go a little further in," Sergei says, and you do so. You light the torch and look down at your little, old friend. He looks peaceful, except for the knife wounds that leave his face a mess of ribbons.

"How do goblins deal with their dead?" you ask Sergei.

"They eat them."

"Oh. Well, how do kabouters do it?"

"We rip them into pieces and play a game with their limbs as bats and their head as a ball."

"Okay, well, we're not doing that, either. We'll do what my friends do."

"What's that?"

You set the torch down and go through A'gog's pockets, taking all of his valuables. A lighter, a small pouch of strange red rocks, and a leather-bound journal.

"We take his stuff, and then we get drunk, and then, I dunno, I guess we just leave him here."

"Alright," Sergei says, respecting your culture. You pass your last flask—from your boot—and the two of you get tipsy.

"Now what?" you ask.

"You said we just leave him here," Sergei replies.

"No, no. Now what do *we* do? Do we wait here?"

"No, my friend. Our part in this struggle is done. We are wanted kabouters. Well, I'm a wanted kabouter. You're a wanted human."

"So, can you help me find my way back aboveground, back to my home?"

Sergei looks at you, a startling gesture since his eyes cannot see. "No, no. My dear Gregory, you can never go home. The gnomes will find you, and they will kill you. Or, of course, do much worse things to you. But if you would like to see the sun again—"

You nod, then, realizing he can't see you, interrupt him by saying, "Yes, I would like to see the sun again."

"Then we will go to Siberia. It's a long journey, but we have comrades there who will hide you. The gnomes cannot abide the cold."

You keep your *own* opinions about the cold—which are quite negative—to yourself because you realize this might be your only chance to survive.

"We will walk for a week until we come to the great conveyance. Conveyance? This isn't the right word. Conveyor, perhaps. The great conveyor, built when the gnomes and the kabouters first came to these lands. It will take us all the way to the cave sea, where we will charter a boat that will take us to Siberia. By this time three months from now, we'll be there and you'll have your sunshine."

Somehow, you're not convinced you would have followed A'gog down the steps in your tower if you'd known what laid ahead of you.

After three days of hiking and crawling through tunnels, hallways, and weird small holes, you're out of torches to burn.

"We should rest here for a few days, until I can produce more snot-torches," Sergei says. "It is pitch dark. You are likely to be eaten by a grue."

"What is a grue?" you ask.

"The grue is a sinister, lurking presence in the dark places of the earth. Its favorite diet is humans," he says. "It doesn't eat kabouters, because fifty thousand years ago, we were the same species. But where we evolved to be civil, the grue evolved as a creature of instinct and violence. We speak of the grue to scare our children, to show them what monsters we might become if we don't conform to society."

*To stay put long enough for Sergei to blow his nose enough for there to be light, go to* **One Hundred and Six** *(page 150).*

*To reject the story as baseless fancy and to hurry on so you might once again see daylight, go to* **One Hundred and Eleven** *(page 156).*

## One Hundred and Two

You throw yourself onto the top bunk, mumble "goodnight," and are asleep before the light is turned off.

Some unknown number of hours later, you awaken refreshed—and still fully clothed. You climb down from the top bunk and begin to walk toward the door when you hear your name called from behind you.

You turn and see the human woman sitting on the bottom bunk, lacing her boots. Her hair is short and black, her skin a light olive, and she appears to be five or so years your senior.

Much like the gnomes, she too wears a plain pair of coveralls, although it is clear that hers are hand-stitched.

"When'd you show up down here?" she asks, her voice gruff and unfriendly, her accent clearly Castilian.

"Last night. At least, I think it was last night." You pull on your watch chain. "My watch is broken," you remark.

"Like I care. You from the city above?"

"Of course. Aren't you?"

"No. I was living in England before I was kidnapped by the gnomes."

"How long ago was that?"

The woman finishes lacing her boots and stands up. "I'll show you where the cafeteria is. Hurry up."

"What's your name?" you ask.

"Comrade Difference Engine."

"What's that?"

"Let's go." Difference Engine walks past you, opens the door, and strides into the hallway, leaving you little choice but to follow. She turns a corner and opens an unmarked door. Behind this is a large room occupied by three dozen of the shorter people, mostly gnomes.

Comrade Difference Engine walks to a strange looking boiler set into the back wall, takes a ceramic mug, and operates a spigot on the boiler, pouring a dark liquid into the cup.

She takes a cautious sip, then a hearty swallow. She looks up at you and says: "I'm right uncivil before coffee in the morning, and you'd taken my usual bed. I'm sorry."

*Go to* **One Hundred and Nine** *(page 154).*

## One Hundred and Three

"A'gog!" you shout. "The torch!"

"What?" A'gog asks.

"You have to light the torch! It's our only chance!"

The torch is lit and suddenly you can see. It's as though the room is made of ice, without seams or masonry, without hard edges or corners. The room is an irregular circle, and perhaps a dozen kabouters sit at a table that protrudes from the floor on chairs that are, of course, a part of the room as well.

But unlike a cavern of ice, this room is flammable, and within moments the walls are burning. Sergei shouts something at you that you haven't time to ponder.

"Run!" you shout, but you needn't have. Everyone in the room understands what to do.

You flee down the hallway and out into the city, the flames on your heels. By the time you're out onto the street, other buildings have caught fire, and you run madly towards what you hope to be the rope ladder and your escape. Your long legs help you outpace your pursuit—and with it, your comrades.

You never turn to look back. You find the ladder and scramble up it, your muscles angrier than they've ever been. Three-quarters the way up the ladder, you turn, expecting to see the city in flames. But instead, the fire has mysteriously gone dead. Then it occurs to you—a fire needs oxygen, which is in limited supply in the cavern. After scorching a good bit of the city, the fire suffocated. Light-headed, you rush to the top of the ladder and through the hatch before you join the blaze in death.

Suddenly, oxygen fills your lungs after the thin, fire-choked air in the city below, and you pass out.

When you come to, you wish you'd perished below. But you strengthen your resolve with alcohol and crawl until you come to a hallway.

You wander the tunnels for hours before you find the steps to your tower. The passageway under the stairs slams shut behind you, trapping you in the world above, and you make your way to your room before falling unconscious once more.

Then, the next morning, you wake up quite sober and deliriously unhappy.

"There are more than 10,000 of us who live in this city, and now we will all die." That is what Sergei had screamed at you as you'd fled. You weep.

Worse, you've lost your hat.

**The End**

## One Hundred and Four

"You don't have to do that," you say to her as she drops the rifle and ties her cane across her back.

She doesn't respond. Instead she crawls out onto the rope and begins to descend. She makes it about halfway before the she is spotted and is shot with a beam of purple light. She holds on for a few seconds as her mouth expresses excruciating pain, but eventually she drops down to the cobbles below.

For some reason, you don't hear her hit, though you see it. Grimly, you watch through the spyglass as she lies unmoving on the pavement, bones splintered and piercing her skin. Then you realize that you've been seen, and soon the air is alive with beams of pain that seek to find you.

Fortunately, they appear to have no effect on the envelope or the basket, so you untie the tether and drift slowly away.

You're uncertain where to go. You decide to leave the city, but after that, you've few ideas. All you have is a balloon, a rifle, and your sorrow. You desperately miss your flask of brandy.

And yet, the world awaits.

**The End**


## One Hundred and Five

You return to the council and sit once more upon the throne at the behest of the councilgnomes.

"You've seen a bit of the city. Not as much as you'll be seeing in the days to come, of course. But enough to understand who we are. Enough to understand our motives, I hope? To know that we seek only to educate, to illuminate. We want to work *with* the goblins, and we hope you'll help us do that."

*To tell the council, in all earnestness, that you intend to help find some kind of compromise between their interests and the interests of the goblins, go to* **One Hundred and Thirteen** *(page 158).*

*To tell the council everything you know of the goblin's plans to attack Hak'kal, such as the strange device in your clock tower, go to* **One Hundred and Fifteen** *(page 160).*

*To pretend to work with the council, but instead spy on them and report to the Aboveground, go to* **One Hundred and Seventeen** *(page 163).*

## One Hundred and Six

"Very well then," you say, "you've sold me. We'll wait a couple of days."

You hadn't been talking much on your hike, mostly because you'd been exhausted, and quite unhappy about the forced period of sobriety. But you spend two days or so talking to keep the darkness at bay.

"I learned about these tunnels from my namesake," Sergei tells you. "A clever man. Taught me Russian and English, and taught me everything I know about guerilla warfare. He escaped Russia, made it all the way to England. He's a writer there now. I think you'd like him."

"What was his name?" you ask.

"Sergei," Sergei says.

"Oh," you say. "Right."

You tell him all about your life, about looking up to your brother—the wild-eyed revolutionary—but being, by and large, more enamored with absinthe and sin than pistols.

"Well, if he saw you now, he'd be proud of you," Sergei says, and those words make you feel both warm and lonely all at once.

Eventually, your stock of torches is renewed and you cross two continents with Sergei. The great conveyor is like something out of a factory, a belt set across wheels. But it runs for a thousand miles, and you are on it for a week. Sergei explains that it is powered by a Stirling engine run off of heat from cracks in the earth. You keep your ignorance of such mechanics to yourself.

Eventually, you come to the underground shore of a vast sea, and a town populated by humans, goblins, gnomes, and kabouters—all of whom seem to live in peace with one another.

A beautiful stranger walks past, and you beg Sergei to stay in exile here, in this fantastical place, well lit and on the shore of the most impressive sea you've ever imagined.

"If we ask the townspeople to hide us," he says, "they will. And then the gnomes will come, and everyone here will die."

"Oh," you say, and charter a small boat powered by a propeller that even Sergei can't explain to you. The trip goes slowly, but it is peaceful out on the water. The fish make for fine eating, and the crew of the boat has excellent taste in wine.

Nearly a month later, you reach the opposite shore, and the crew of the ship wishes you luck, gifting you with beautiful—if strange—clothes and three bottles of wine.

You emerge from the tunnels and are blinded by the light.

"The sun is so bright," you say, "like I would never have imagined!"

"It is nighttime," Sergei says, "I think you're talking about the moon."

"Oh," you say, and eventually your eyes adjust. It's a full moon, the ground is covered in snow, and in the distance is a small village.

"Is that where we're going to live?"

"I figure so," Sergei says. "The Hak'kal Aboveground has connections there. They will shelter us."

"How long do we have to stay?" you ask.

"Until this blows over," Sergei says.

It takes forty years before news reaches you. Sergei has died of old age a decade past. One night, as you sit before the fire, content, finishing your translations of A'gog's journal, a young gnome knocks on your door."

"Mr. Gregory?" he asks, in English, a tongue you haven't spoken aloud in years.

"Yes?"

"I'm from Hak'kal," the gnome says.

"I suppose you've come to kill me?" you ask.

"Oh, heavens. Oh heavens no. I've been sent to tell you the news." And tell you he does: your actions had become legend, and you'd become a folk hero. Finally, two goblin generations later, some young kabouters joined them in their battle, forming a Sergei brigade, and they stormed Hak'kal. The colonialist government was ousted, and worker's councils that represent all the underground races have formed in order to manage the caverns.

"You're a hero, Mr. Gregory," the gnome says.

"A hero?" you answer, "no, my young friend. I am an old man, a terrible drunk, and thrice divorced. If there was ever a hero, his story is here." You hand A'gog's diary to the emissary.

"Will you come back with me to Hak'kal?"

"Oh, oh dear. I'll come, but just to visit."

So once again you cross the underground sea. But after attending a brief ceremony in Hak'kal—a city so war-torn so as to look more like a natural cave than a city—you find your way back to the town on the water's edge and find yourself work as a fisher, where you stay until your natural death, many years later.

### The End

### One Hundred and Seven

You shove Emile across the street with surprising force, knocking him over in the process. But a moment later, the leaping assailant lands her wrench just where his head had been. Which is, quite unfortunately, where your arm still is.

You have only a moment to think about the pain, fortunately.

"*Vas te faire enculer, porc-dog*," the goblin says, snarling. She brings her wrench around and up into your genitals, dropping you in surprise, then she stabs the end of the wrench into your eyes. Shortly thereafter, your brain is utterly destroyed, and you die.

You die in the process of trying to keep a slave from liberation, you die in defense of colonialism and all that is proper, all that is tea and biscuits and empire. In short, you die the worst possible death one could possibly imagine.

**The End**

### One Hundred and Eight

"You lowly mushroom!" Gu'dal yells at you, "You pestilent gnome-fornicator! You, you... you child of unmarried parents!"

You drift away from the scene of the slaughter, numb. You pile more and more fuel upon the flames, drifting up to where the air is so thin you're unable to focus on your guilt at having survived the battle, your sorrow for losing. The swift winds of the upper sky drag you quickly away, and when you eventually run out of fuel and descend you are at the edge of abandoned farmlands, near a great forest.

It turns out that goblins cry tears of blood, and Gu'dal's face is as macabre a sight as any you've seen.

But stoically, she marches into the forest and returns dragging a dead deer. You make a fire and eat, still silent.

Then you sleep for the whole of the night and much of the next day. When you awake, Gu'dal has gathered fuel for the balloon.

"Where to?" you ask.

"I don't think I've a home to return to. And I've the feeling you haven't either."

You nod.

"Then it doesn't really matter where we go, now does it? Our lot will be cast with the winds."

You smile, something you rarely do while sober. You've a rifle, a balloon, and a fierce goblin for a companion. The world awaits you.

**The End**

**One Hundred and Nine**

Comrade Pneumatic H. Fourteen invites the two of you over to an intricate stonework table. The ceiling of the cafeteria is arched, like a typical subterranean bar.

"Why are most of the hallways and buildings down here built to human scale?" you ask the gnome, "They must seem gigantic to you."

"No, no," Pneumatic responds, "when you live your life underground, you learn to appreciate vertical space. If you can jump and hit your head on the ceiling, it's too low. If your feet have to touch the ground when you're sitting on a chair, it's too short. That's how we gnomes design."

"Alright," you nod.

"Any other questions?" Pneumatic asks.

"Why'd you risk rescuing me?" you ask.

"Know what they do with humans?" Comrade Difference Engine responds.

You shake your head.

"You've heard the voices from the dark sky above, yes? The operas and ballads and bawdy drinking songs in all the languages of the above-worlds?"

You nod. "Only humans know how to work the machines then? Or they use humans to gather the musical recordings somehow?"

"No. There are no machines. The ceiling is draped with a hundred birdcages. In each cage squats a naked human, singing for their supper." Difference sips at her coffee, failing to conceal her anger.

"I don't believe it," you say, because you don't. It is simply too much. The gnomes seem so cheerful and kind, present company included.

"It's true. They enslave the goblins, they enslave the kabouters..." Difference notices your look of confusion. "The kabouters are the blind ones. They see by echolocation. The gnomes brought them here when they first built the city. They've been slaves to the gnomes for their entire cultural memory."

Eleven gets up from the table and returns with large bowl filled with a gray paste. Each of your companions takes turns with a metal straw, sucking down breakfast. You try it, and it's not as bad as you fear. The texture makes you want to puke a little, but the taste is complex and lovely.

"So now that you're here, how would you like to help?" Pneumatic asks.

"Well, I've got a couple ideas," you say, even though you don't.

Everyone looks at you expectantly and you attempt to rattle your brain into thinking.

*To say, "Have you any photographic equipment? I'll create daguerreotypes of the cages and wield them as evidence. Once the press spreads the word, the government will be forced into action." go to* **One Hundred and Fourteen** *(page 158).*

*To suggest that they return you to the surface, so that you may enlist the help of the subversives you know through your brother, go to* **One Hundred and Sixteen** *(page 161).*

*To ask to see what in Hak'kal might be susceptible to sabotage, go to* **One Hundred and Eighteen** *(page 165).*

## One Hundred and Ten

You take a step back and watch as the goblin lands her wrench directly on the crown of Emile's head, caving it in with a single blow. She casts the blood off the head of her tool as though it were a sword—by giving it a quick swish through the air—and takes off running, deeper into the engineering district.

No one follows. Everyone is too stunned. No gnome cries, no goblin cheers. Somehow, the general peace is unbroken. But, of course, for Emile, who lies dead at your feet.

Clearly, things are not as simple as the council has led you to believe. You take a flask out of your boot and drink deeply before wandering back towards the council building.

*Go to* **One Hundred and Five** *(page 149).*

## One Hundred and Eleven

"We have stories like that on the surface," you tell Sergei. "We tell our children about vampires and other horrors, of people that eat people and hide from the sun. And we tell our children to obey, to always stay in sight. And when they grow up? To obey the police, to always stay within civilization or they'll be eaten by bogeymen. And it's nonsense. So no, thank you for the warning, but I'll be quite content to be on our way, to get to my cold exile in frozen Siberia." It occurs to you that you're being quite harsh, but you haven't eaten much, haven't had a drink days, and are quite frustrated.

"Have it your way," Sergei says, and you continue on.

You hear feet stampeding towards you, and a screech goes out in the dark.

"That wasn't me," Sergei says.

But you can't answer him. You have been eaten by a grue.

**The End**

## One Hundred and Twelve

You pull on a leather glove and throw burning fuel down onto the gnomes gathered below. Soon, the balloon begins to sink.

Gu'dal looks at you and smiles. You crouch next to her, up against the wall of the basket, waiting to take the gnomes by surprise.

When you hit the ground, the gnomes rush you. The first over the wall of the basket is stabbed through the throat by Gu'dal, the next is blinded when you shatter the smoky glass of his helmet.

You grab a dropped lightrifle and begin to fire. But of course, you are soon overwhelmed. When you die, bludgeoned by clubs and rifle-butts, your last sight is of Gu'dal, viscously lashing out with cane, blade, and teeth, killing those who enslaved her people. Pain dulled by adrenaline, you smile and fall into death.

**The End**

### One Hundred and Thirteen

"I would hate to see bloodshed," you tell the council. *Because I'm quite squeamish* is a bit that you keep to yourself.

And so you spend the next five days hashing out plans to reform relations between the gnomes and goblins. The goblins are to be paid wages for their work, and they will be able to elect a single councilgoblin from among their ranks—in an observational post. You advocate strongly for several key points that would otherwise have been left out of the plan, such as a guarantee of food for every goblin who is physically unable to work.

You have to make compromises, of course. You had hoped they would include the freedom of travel for goblins, but it had been shot down. In exchange, they conceded to grant leave to qualified goblins, amounting to one day in every five-day. No small thing, you decide, self-assuredly.

When the Goblin Liberation Act is signed into law, you are allowed to co-sign "on behalf of goblins," and your heart swells with pride.

Six months later, the sonalopticloopticamplificator destroys a large chunk of Hak'kal, and angry—ungrateful—goblin workers storm the city. They find you sitting on your throne in the council building and take you outside. They charge you with collaboration, put you up against the wall, and shoot you.

### The End

### One Hundred and Fourteen

Pneumatic objects: "So we involve the humans? What then? The human governments take over the caverns? What improves?"

"To say that all humans are bad is as useless as saying all *gnomes* are bad," Difference replies, "is it not?"

"All gnomes *are* bad," says the gnome. "Certainly, I'm trying to kill the colonialist in my head, but I never can, not completely. I don't know that humans are any better. Only the goblins and the kabouters, they bear none of this sickness. Pure and noble. But I suppose the enemy of my enemy... oh, hell."

"Well, do you have photographic equipment or not?" you ask.

"I'm afraid we don't. The photographic process is a closely guarded secret among us, and only very few are trusted with the power of the camera-plate."

"I suppose I shall have to return to the surface and acquire the equipment myself, then."

Comrade Difference Engine shows you to a tunnel that deposits you in a canal. You swim to the surface and climb up to the street, oblivious, in your haste, of the sewage odor that lingers in your sopping clothes.

You hurry back to your apartment and gather everything you own of worth. You hesitate as you reach for your grandmother's wedding band, but the mournful caged voices come into your head. You find your way to the pawnshop and exchange your meager inheritance for a camera and plates.

You throw the whole of the equipment into a large rucksack and hurry back to your clock tower home, where it hits you, cold as sobriety: the passageway under the steps is no more. You find no trace, no tell-tale edge.

You return to your apartment and stare at the empty glass bottles that line your shelves, tables, and floor.

Perhaps, you decide, it would be prudent to return the camera equipment and purchase more alcohol. If the world of adventure and cunning and revolution is locked forever from you, then oblivion seems your only option.

**The End**


## One Hundred and Fifteen

The council listens with rapt attention to you—or rather, your interpreter—as you tell them about the goblin's plan to raid Hak'kal, about the Soniloopi… the Sonaloptica… the uh, the weird contraption they're building in your belfry.

As soon as you're done talking, they burst into speech, all of them at once. Strangely, it looks as though they are actually capable of listening at the same time as they speak—an ability that many of your "intellectual" companions claim to have, but of course do not.

Unfortunately, most of the conversation happens in Gnomish, but the interpreter manages to let you in on some of the more interesting bits.

"How can the goblins be so ungrateful… of course they are upset, we need to show more good faith… it's time that we squished them between our teeth like rocks… the important thing is that the attack didn't happen… make an example." And so forth, for the better part of a half-hour, before your eyes begin to glaze over.

"Would you like dinner?" your interpreter asks you.

And for the first time in a good long while, you grin. Dinner sounds lovely.

A guard is summoned into the room and escorts you out, but you have the impression that he is there as a guide and not as a captor. You are led to a restaurant, an elegant place with crystal chandeliers—in which the crystals themselves do the lighting!—and tables suited for a man of your stature. None of the other tables are occupied, and once you sit down, your guard leaves.

A waiter comes out and speaks to you in French. Fortunately, your minor command of the language allows you to request dinner and wine.

This is served shortly, by a different waiter, a strikingly handsome one. It is only once you've begun to sip at your wine that you recognize him—he is the gnome who threatened you the night before! And now he stands before you, a smirk pasted across his face, and you have drunk his poison!

"*Bon appetite, vous porcs impérialistes.*"

It's a strange feeling, a bit like a fever. Unfortunately, it's nothing like opium. You had always hoped that death would be a welcome embrace, like poppy. But it's not. It's insufferable. And it goes on, and on. Forever.

**The End**

**One Hundred and Sixteen**

Pneumatic doesn't sound convinced. "So we involve humans in our business now? What good are humans? Why would they care?"

Difference replies to the gnome: "What about the cages on the ceiling?"

"What about them? What does entertainment have to do with anything?"

"*Entertainment?!*" Comrade Difference Engine is outraged, and Pneumatic quickly looks meek, realizing the depths of her error.

You interject into the argument. "I know they'll help. My brother's friends. They can get us weapons, bombs. Oh, we'll take down Hak'kal," you say, your voice quivering with possibility, "whatever the cost."

Your companions look at you queerly but they help you prepare for your trip. You return to the daylight by means of a tunnel that deposits you into a canal. You swim to the surface and climb up to the street, reeking of the foul city water.

Searching your way through your hazy memories, you find the basement club where your brother and his compatriots (comrades, he called them, like the Aboveground) had met before his deportment to the prison colonies.

Inside, the bar looks like a crypt, with low arched ceilings and walls of exposed stonework. Opium smoke fills the air, but you recognize the large-mustachioed face of Victor, your brother's friend, at the back of the club, talking with a mad sobriety with two serious-faced women.

"Explosives," you say, approaching the trio, "and firearms. I need to procure guns." You sit down in an empty chair and interrupt their conversation.

"Gregory! I haven't seen your face for some time! I must say, you look the worse for wear–" Victor begins.

"Of course, of course, where are my manners?" you turn and introduce yourself to the two women. "Niceties accomplished. I need a lot of gunpowder. It's a matter of life and death."

"For whom?" one of the women, who wears the clothing of a poor man, asks you.

*To lie and speak of your concern for the fate of your lost brother,* go to **One Hundred and Twenty** *(page 168).*

*To speak candidly of the city of Hak'kal below the sunlit streets, go to* **One Hundred and Twenty-Two** *(page 171).*

## One Hundred and Seventeen

"I'm quite interested in helping you resolve this situation as amicably as possible," you say, the lies tasting welcome on your lips, like whisky.

The council outlines their plans for the "emancipation" of their goblin slaves while you listen intently. What might otherwise be tedious to a man of your slothful temperament is dreadfully interesting when it has become intrigue, you realize. You also realize that their plans to "free" the goblins are, well, just another stage in the imperialist process—as your brother used to say. They plan on letting the goblins elect their own leaders to report to the gnomes, even let the goblins have their own police force that can punish other goblins.

After an hour or so, a guard escorts you to a downright fancy French restaurant, where you are told to order anything that pleases you, courtesy of the council. The tables are suited for a person of your height, there are no other patrons, and even the guard leaves to allow you privacy. When the waiter comes out and takes your order of wine, you smile. The life of a spy is a good one, you decide.

The waiter who brings you your food is remarkably attractive, for a gnome. Then, as the wine is placed in front of you, you recognize him—the gnome who offered to rescue you, last night!

"What a coincidence that you work here," you say, because you are not sly.

"What is this word?" the waiter asks.

"Nevermind," you say.

"Do you bring information?"

And you let him know the council's plans. Your contact nods, listening patiently, even as you take the story off on tangents, like your tour of the city.

"It is good thing you have been coming to the Hak'kal," he says, and waits for you to figure out what the hell he's talking about. "You study information well. The Imperialist swine will give us money for what they have done!" He looks uncertain. "'Give us money,' this is a phrase you would use, yes?"

"I think you mean 'pay.'"

"I am confused. 'Give us money' and 'pay,' they mean the same, yes?"

You try to explain the difference, but it's hard, so you drink wine instead.

"It is nothing. What is important is that you study more information. I think the council will let you be alive for a five-day, at very least. You have a five-day to study all the information. Study how much soldiers they will have on goblins when the goblins are let to be goblin-police."

"They're going to kill me?" you ask, not paying nearly as much attention to the rest of what the waiter-spy-gnome had said.

"Of course they will kill you. Or put you in cage and make you sing, above Hak'kal. You will not be *useful*. And you will to have been studying so much. These councilgnomes, they will have red cheeks, yes, but they will have white teeth. This is what we say. Red cheeks but white teeth."

You want to argue with him, but only because the wine is getting to you and you don't want the councilgnomes to be trying to kill you. Instead you wait for your meal, eat somberly, and say farewell to your contact.

"I will visit you all nights," he says, "and will make you free when you say. Not free like council says goblins are free. But free like… free like bat in a cave is free."

And he is true to his confusing word. Every day you sit on the throne at the council and listen attentively. You ask strategic questions, slowly tricking the council into feeding you new information. Every night, your handsome friend slips in the window of your room and you relay everything you've heard.

On the fourth day in front of the council, the conversation is more heated than usual, and your interpreter tells you very little. A few times, you hear your name in the conversation. The old, aristocratic councilgnome looks at you meets your eyes, and spits.

That night you decide to escape.

"Of course," your Aboveground contact says, "where would you like to go?"

*To be escorted back to the surface, where so many letters sit unanswered at your desk, go to* **One Hundred and Nineteen** *(page 166).*

*To join the Aboveground, go to* **One Hundred and Twenty-One** *(page 170).*

## One Hundred and Eighteen

"We must make total destroy on the center boiler. This will make the victory of the proletariat. An impossible attack at the heart of empire." Comrade Eleven Stroke B. speaks enthusiastically, clutching at the table.

But Comrade Pneumatic H. Fourteen voices a different opinion: "The central pneumatic exchange chamber controls all of our enemy's communications. We should take you there to cautiously observe."

"It is not talking that we must stop! It is power!" Eleven gets out of his chair and begins to jump up and down on the table, casting dark gazes at Pneumatic. "We talk, they talk. Talk is like the empty space. Talk is nothing!"

Pneumatic looks to you.

*To side with Comrade Eleven Stroke B. with the intention of staging an attack on the central boiler of Hak'kal, go to* **One Hundred and Twenty-Three** *(page 172).*

*To side with Comrade Pneumatic H. Fourteen and see what can be done to interrupt Hak'kal's communications, go to* **One Hundred and Twenty-Four** *(page 174).*

## One Hundred and Nineteen

"With me," the gnome says, then vaults out the window, cute as a kitten.

You follow, and the two of you take off at a run. Although you lack his endurance, your longer legs do make you the faster runner.

And suddenly, speed becomes important, because a beam of purple light cuts through the dark air above your head.

"Run!" the gnome says, although you are already at a sprint.

You chance a look over your shoulder and see a score of riflegnomes in pursuit. You run faster.

Suddenly a gnome's arm reaches out from an alley and pulls you in. "Now run this way," the new gnome—a shorter-than-average woman with spiky red hair—says.

The comely fellow is gone, as he kept running. You don't know if the trade-off was for your safety or his, but you decide to follow this new gnome as she runs through the maze-like city. You are approaching the edge of the cavern, you realize, because the roof is suddenly visible and is dropping quite rapidly as you flee your pursuit.

Soon, you have to crouch. But your companion reaches up to the ceiling and pulls down a step-ladder hatch—like those that lead to attics—and shoves you quite rudely up it. She follows and pulls it shut.

The hall is dark, lit only by a softly glowing fungus. Your rescuer takes you by the hand and leads you, jogging, as you fight to keep your breath. You are clearly going uphill.

You finally stop at a slow-moving river.

"In," the gnome says, gesturing towards the river.

"Why? Will that take me home?"

But it's clear that your companion doesn't speak English.

You stand your full height, stretch your tired muscles, catch your breath, and jump in. You long ago learned that, once you knew you would do something, it was best to simply do it and not waste time with fear or uncertainty. It's just that, usually, you apply this to such practical pursuits as subsistence theft or hallucinogenic experimentation.

The water is cold, but not as cold as you'd feared, and suddenly you see daylight ahead. You swim for it, and emerge in a canal, the sun above you.

You laugh heartily, laugh as you fight for breath and paddle to stay afloat. You laugh so hard that you attract attention to yourself, and a crowd forms along the bank of the canal.

But what is one more madman in the water, you ask. What care do I have for the opinion of the useless, pampered gentry?

You swim to shore and trudge through the streets of your adopted city, soaking, shivering, and deliriously happy.

Back at your tower, you head into your room to change and find a chunk of gold the size of your fist sitting on your table. Under it, an unsigned note reads:

*Thanks for everything. The pugilists will take it from here. If… no… when* we win, *we'll stop by and thank you in person.*

You weigh the chunk of gold in your hand. First, you think, you'll get a drink. Then, maybe, it's time to see the world.

### The End

### One Hundred and Twenty

"Er… my brother."

"You mean to sail across the ocean to effect his rescue?" Victor asks, clearly impressed.

The two women look confused, and Victor explains: "Remember George, who was nicked for smuggling guns to the African resistance after escaping the destruction of the Paris commune? Meet his brother."

The second woman, wearing the garb of a well-to-do lady, looks at you, impressed.

"I've already arranged passage for myself," you explain, "but I need a trunk full of firearms, to uh… arm the prisoners, and another trunk of bombs. Demolition, you must understand."

"They are yours," the woman who is dressed as a woman says.

"As simple as that?" the woman who is dressed as a man asks.

"As simple as that. A more noble cause I've never imagined. To sail across the ocean to rescue his kin?"

"Well, that there's your answer," Victor says.

You return to your home by a circuitous route, in fear that your footsteps might be dogged by the secret police, and wait in the shadows for a few hours. As the bells above toll eleven, a carriage makes its way up the cobbles, and, as instructed, you retrieve two wooden trunks and carry them with care into your tower. The locks are ornate, the wood well-oiled, and it is clear to you that the trunks alone would fetch a healthy sum.

It's only once you stand at the foot of the stairs that it strikes you: the passageway is gone. You run to your room and return with a magnifying glass, but can find no crack, no disturbed mortar.

Frustrated, you set explosives by the wall, trusting blindly to intuition to guide you through their placement and handling. The demolition goes smoothly, but you find no passageway in the rubble. What's more, you have little time to look, as you are certain the authorities will respond to your midnight blasting.

Your mind pumped full of adrenaline, you make a split-second decision. The way to your room is blocked, so you make your way to the docks with only your two heavy trunks of firepower.

Thereupon, you buy passage for the colonies by trading an ornate rifle. You have learned one thing from your stay with the little races, fictional it may have been: oppression need not be tolerated. Your brother will be free, you decide, or your life will be forfeit in the attempt.

**The End**

## One Hundred and Twenty-One

"Follow," the gnome says, then vaults out the window.

You try to mimic his grace, but manage to fall hard on your shoulder. Your hat takes off, rolling down the street, and you move to chase it.

Ten paces later, it's in your hand, and you right it on your head. Then you look over to see your would-be-rescuer being chased by nearly a score of lightrifle-wielding gnomes.

You exclaim something inappropriate, perhaps something referring to intercourse or excrement, and—in an act most unfitting of your pre-spy nature—sprint *towards* the fuss.

You pass the gnomes handily, owing to your longer legs, and swoop up your friend in your arms. Adrenaline courses through your veins—as good as the orangutan stuff you sometimes buy—and you outpace your pursuit as beams of purple light scatter about you against the wall and street.

Until a sharp pain runs up through your leg and you stumble, dropping your friend and smashing your face on the cobbles. You've been shot, you realize.

And although you survive that encounter—thanks to a remarkable bit of stone-throwing by your companion—, it certainly isn't the last time the purple beam hits and hurts you.

You spend the next six months of your life fighting as part of the gnomish Aboveground, raiding and skirmishing against the authorities. You fight alongside creatures of every sentient species, but it isn't a war that is won overnight. It's not until six months pass, and the sonalopticloopticamplificator is activated, that the goblins are able to overrun Hak'kal.

Unfortunately, you're killed in that battle.

### The End

## One Hundred and Twenty-Two

"Well, you see, there are these gnomes…" You explain, in frightening detail, your adventures over the past—how long has it been since you went underground? You cannot recall.

Although the woman dressed as a man looks at you incredulously, and Victor's face is completely unreadable, you recognize that the second woman, who is in the garb of a well-to-do lady, believes you.

"What utter shit," the woman dressed as a man says.

"You can have the weapons," the woman dressed as a woman says.

"What? You can't be serious! Gnomes, kabouters? Goblins?!"

"It's my money what buys the guns, and I suggest we donate them to this gentleman."

You look to your proponent graciously, and she smiles.

"*Your* money?! *Your* money? Just because your father is the goddam–" the poor woman begins, but cuts herself off before she reveals her comrade's identity, "does not make it *your* money. It is the Underground's money."

Victor sighs. "We'll give him the guns. I don't believe him any more than you, but it's better to sacrifice two trunks of munitions than lose our source, you must understand."

The poor woman crosses her arms, but says no more.

You pick your way back home carefully, doubling back quite often to make life difficult for anyone who might be tailing you. You wait anxiously in the dark, and as the bells above you strike eleven, a carriage trots up. As instructed, you remove two expensive wooden trunks from the empty carriage, and the driver nods at you before driving off.

But as you step inside your clock tower, you realize that you cannot find the passageway under the stairs. You go over every inch of stonework, to no avail. Perhaps it was all fantasy.

Instinct drives your hand into your pocket, reaching for a flask. But a new thought creeps into your mind. Perhaps it was all a dream of your feverish and drugged mind, but you've learned from it regardless.

You've all the munitions to stage a slave rebellion.

You wait for dawn, then proceed to the docks, trading an expensive pair of pistols for passage to the colonies. Your brother will be free, you decide, or else your body will lie beside his in some shallow tropical grave.

**The End**

## One Hundred and Twenty-Three

You look around the breakfast table. "I suppose the thing to do is get this business over with as swiftly as possible, so that, vow to the goblins sated, I may return to my correspondence in the world above. And besides, I may be hallucinating, but the rulers of Hak'kal have gone too far. Give me a gun and a wrench and a bit of a plan."

Eleven looks at you from where he stands on the table. "I can use you for riflegnome today," he says, "we will make the attack. And we will make total destroy!"

"What?!" Comrade Pneumatic H. Fourteen shouts, "No! Are you crazy? The Aboveground can't afford to lose *anyone* in a frivolous attack on an impossible target! It was bad enough when you left last night to rescue that useless…" She gains control of her voice. "I simply won't have it. No one will come with you."

"Autonomy!" Comrade Eleven Stroke B. declares, hopping down to stand on his chair. "You will not stop me or new riflegnome from the glorious attack we will make! Tomorrow, when freedom day, you will say many thanks! You have no brain-strength! When you place many fires in building, the building may burn. When you place no fires, nothing!"

He hops down from the chair. "I go to the armory."

You stand up, bid your company adieu, and set off after Eleven.

The armory, as it turns out, is nearly empty. A single light-rifle is held on a rack on the wall. A half-dozen slingshots sit on a cabinet that is next to a small barrel of rocks that is next to a hot-water heater—the armory clearly serving a double purpose.

High on the wall, clearly in the place of honor, is a hand-crafted and exquisitely designed weapon that reminds you of nothing you've ever fancied. The barrel is of steel as bright as silver, both enameled and engraved with hieroglyphic writing. The stock seems carved of ivory. Sprouting haphazardly at all angles are the most complex crystal and mirror workings you have yet seen.

"Is that the—" you begin.

"Eleven Stroke B."

Eleven picks up his namesake, and you admire it for another moment before he tells you to take the lightrifle.

"You are riflegnome. I am saboteur. If you see gnome with helmet or rifle, you shoot them. Don't shoot them in the armor. Only Eleven Stroke B. will shoot them in the armor. You follow?"

You nod.

"Good. When you die, you die like gnome, like goblin, like kabouter. Like human. But maybe you don't die today. Maybe today is victory."

You take a pull from your flask and follow Comrade Eleven Stroke B. out through a labyrinth of work tunnels. Soon, everything is pitch black, and you follow the sound of gnome footsteps.

A door opens, you step through, and hear a scream. The last thing you see is a beam of purple striking your comrade, and the searing microwave heat of a ray-weapon drives into your back. You collapse, like a gnome, like a goblin, like a kabouter, or like a human. Most of all, you collapse like so much meat, dead and cooking.

**The End**

## One Hundred and Twenty-Four

"An empire cannot stand without communications, or so my brother always said when we were little. Of course, he was justifying his theft of stationary from the post office. But regardless, let us go to the central exchange." You stand, straighten your bowler, and look to your company. Eleven shakes his head and heads off with the remainder of the breakfast bowl, leaving you with Pneumatic and Difference.

"Right then, to the ventilation system," Pneumatic says, and leaves the cafeteria for the hallway outside.

"It's a bit cramped for us tall folk," Difference apologizes.

The two women lead you to a vent grill as tall as your waist. Pneumatic unlatches an innumerable series of locks and catches, and the vent swings open. Inside is darkness and wind.

"Just follow me," the gnome says.

You crouch down to hands and knees and crawl into the air vent after Pneumatic. Difference enters behind you.

"We can get to most any part of Hak'kal this way," Pneumatic explains, her voice echoing metallic, "it's how the Aboveground operates."

"What exactly is it that you all do?" you ask.

"Oh, plotting and planning, mostly. Sometimes we sabotage works in progress. A few decades back we staged a raid on a goblin work camp, freed some folk, found them new homes."

"A few *decades* ago? How long has the Aboveground been around?"

"There's always been the Aboveground. As long as there has been empire, we've been around to contest it."

"Lot of good it's done anyone," you whisper. If anyone heard, they made no remark.

Occasional light filters in through vents set into the side of the tunnel, but you haven't the time to stop to peer out. Your guide, able to walk freely, is clearly impatient at waiting for you to clamber along behind. For the most part, you are crawling in utter darkness, following the sound of footsteps. You turn a few times, moving up and down shallow inclines.

The better part of an aching, muscle-torturing hour later, Pneumatic stops in front of a grill set into the tunnel wall and puts her face against it to see through. You catch up, and do likewise.

It's as though you are looking at the guts of a massive animal: the twisted intestines of metal tubing, curving organically, surrounded by glass arteries through which pump pneumatic canisters, expanding well past your limited field of vision.

"This is it," Pneumatic whispers, "the central hub of their communication networks. Some of these pipes run for leagues… out to the fungus farms, the mines, even the surface collaborators. It's pretty well guarded."

"How well guarded?" you ask.

"A patrol comes through every fifteen minutes or so."

"You thinking what I'm thinking?"

"I don't see how that would be possible. We have two completely different contexts. That's why I thought to bring you here, really. You're going to think of different things than I am."

"Alright, alright. What we need to do is wait until the guards pass by, and then…"

*To finish your sentence with, "And then find a good-sized stick and begin to bash the machinery into pieces," go to* **One Hundred and Twenty-Five** *(page 176).*

*If you'd rather say, "And then I'll stop up the tubes with uh… with my hat," go to* **One Hundred and Twenty-Six** *(page 178).*

## One Hundred and Twenty-Five

You wait, silent as you are able, for long minutes. The rumble of the machine, the whoosh of canisters and bonk of switches fill the windy air. Finally, a bored trio of gnomes, be-helmeted and armed, crosses from your left to your right.

After they are gone, Pneumatic works quickly with her folding pocketwrench, unbolting the vent. She pushes it forward with great care, setting it down on the stone floor of the machine room.

You burst out, anxious to get on with the work. You've been mucking about tunnels for too long. Your muscles hurt and your brain is tired of this constant hallucinating. It will be nice to be through with it, you decide.

You grab a protruding lever and give it a yank, meaning to pry it free. It slips, and suddenly the canisters begin to travel at a frenzied pace. You curse yourself under your breath for having abandoned your cane. Then you twist the lever, find it loose, and unscrew it from its base.

Ball-headed lever held as a cudgel, you swing at the nearest glass. It shatters with a satisfying pop, glass flying back at your face from the pressurized air within. Your face is cut, and you enter something of a blood-rage, acting as though you had drunk a bottle of spirits to yourself.

Smash and crash and shatter and noise, noise, noise. You barely notice the fear painted on the faces of your hosts as you swing with wild enthusiasm. What you lack in strength—and what you lack in strength is, indeed, a sizable amount—you make up for in sheer insanity. No glass stays unbroken, no brass unbent. You've built up quite a bit of rage, being underground and confused, and finally you have a yielding object to take it out on.

You are stopped only by a searing purple light that cuts across your body with the agony of sunburn. Soon you drop, turning to see that the guards have returned and are shooting you and your friends with their painful lightrifles.

It's possible that your valiant sabotage threw the fascist machinery of the gnomes into chaos, a chaos as virulent to empire as a plague is to humanity. It's possible that the oppressed creatures of the underworld threw off their yokes as the communication systems of their oppressors broke down and rid themselves of Hak'kal for once and all.

But you will never know, because you are dead.

**The End**

## One Hundred and Twenty-Six

You crouch in the noisy darkness, watching canisters fly through tubes. Eventually, three gnomes pace across your line of sight, wearing helmets and bearing lightrifles.

As soon as they're gone, Eleven pulls a folding pocketwrench from her pocket and sets to work opening the grate. It comes loose and she lowers it carefully onto the floor of the central exchange hub.

"Are you certain this will work?" Difference asks you.

"No, of course not. It's a ridiculous plan. But, I figure, I'm crawling through ventilation tunnels nearly a league below the earth, consorting with gnomes and goblins. So really, it seems as possible as anything else."

"Fair enough," Difference replies.

Pneumatic, for her part, looks skeptical and is inspecting the machine.

"Can you open one of these pipes?" you ask the gnome as you walk over to one as thick as your head.

"Of course," Pneumatic says. She applies her pocketwrench to a joint and soon has the pipe in pieces. Air rushes from the bottom half, and soon a heavy brass-and-glass canister pops out and drops to the ground.

You take off your hat and place it into the receiving end of the tube, where suction holds it in place. Pneumatic replaces the joint and you make a hasty retreat, stopping only to grab the heavy canister on the ground.

You heart is racing nearly the entire crawl back to the Aboveground headquarters. The ventilation's wind is now at your back, and even your cramps seem to have disappeared, overwhelmed by the potential immensity of your simple action.

You return to the command center to find it in chaos. Pneumatic is informed immediately that the city's communications are down, and she smiles. A gnome's smile, as you realize, is nothing like a human's, nor a goblin's. A gnome's smile is all teeth, top and bottom, lips pulled back until the red of the gums glint like a drunkard's eyes.

"We have our visitor to thank for that," Pneumatic informs the resistance. "He has single-handedly clogged the entire pneumatic tube network of Hak'kal."

"That was the civil communication as well as the governmental?" you ask.

"Of course, of course. They're all connected. It's a network, a series of tubes. When you try to shove too much information, too many canisters through one clogged tube, the breakdown reverberates throughout the rest. I thought you knew that? Isn't that why you clogged that pipe?"

"Of course," you lie.

For the next several hours, no one is permitted to enter or exit the compound. It's too dangerous, the Aboveground claims. They will sit and wait for information, as they always do.

Finally, a messengergoblin peeks her head through the hatchway in the floor and speaks to the assembled group: "There's a general revolt at the mines."

The Aboveground cheers, a high-pitched chorus, the pure joy of children. According to the messenger, the taskmasters weren't relieved on time, and when half of them went back to Hak'kal to investigate the problem, the workers revolted and seized the weaponry. Hak'kal is surrounded, as the goblins and kabouters lay siege.

Immediately, the room is divided. Half of those present, mostly the gnomes, feel it prudent, or perhaps strategic, to stay put and see how things develop. The other half felt the need to gather arms and join the besieging army.

"How about it?" Difference asks you.

*To indicate that you've done your part but that you must return to the letters that sit unanswered at your desk on the surface, go to* **One Hundred and Twenty-Seven** *(page 180).*

*To announce that you've sat and talked enough already in your life, that you're ready to take gun in hand and join the battle for liberation, go to* **One Hundred and Twenty-Eight** *(page 181).*


### One Hundred and Twenty-Seven

Comrade Difference Engine looks at you. Perhaps she is disappointed, perhaps she is unsurprised. Perhaps she is sad to see you leave. But no emotion crosses her face. "Farewell, then. Return to your letters. If you'd like to reach us, address one to 'Aboveground, Hak'kal,' and a comrade will intercept it."

The strangers in the room bid you a fond farewell, and soon Comrade Eleven Stroke B. leads you through back tunnels and deposits you at the base of the steps to your tower.

"Will you be returning to the Aboveground?" you ask him.

He spits. "You cannot take feathers from a naked chicken, no? The Aboveground? They will put their hands into their... into their, I don't know the word. They will do nothing. But *I* will make total destroy on Hak'kal." He un-shoulders his lightrifle. He salutes with his six-fingered hand, then turns and stalks down the tunnel, whistling a tune whose words you will never know.

You, for your part, return to your room, your wine, your letters, and your bed. You open the pneumatic canister, and try to read the message scrawled within, but it is quite foreign to you. Your thoughts turn to your brother, over in the prison colonies. You ponder his fate, you ponder your own.

You think of how, when your brother was deported so rudely, you said nothing. You were too insignificant. You merely hoped. But perhaps, perhaps you have agency. If you can free the goblins, surely you can free your family. First though, to sleep.

**The End**

**One Hundred and Twenty-Eight**

Comrade Difference Engine, Comrade Eleven Stroke B., the goblins, the kabouters, and yourself scrap together what arms you can and make for the least guarded entrance to the city.

The guards never saw you coming, and soon you add the weapons you pry from their dead hands to those of your own and open the doors to the workers outside the gates.

One door at a time you storm through the city, soft as hummingbirds, swift as lightning, cruel as vengeance. You cut down guards without mercy or thought, open doors to let in wave after wave of angry slaves.

As you approach what you think to be the last door, you're blinded by friendly fire and drop to the ground. By the time your vision is restored, the fight is over.

"Did we win?" you ask a passing goblin. But she cannot speak your language, and she passes by.

"Did we win?" you ask a passing kabouter. But he is bleeding from a clearly soon-to-be-fatal head wound, and pays you no mind.

For nearly an hour you stumble through the strange battle-field, the beautiful streets of Hak'kal littered with the wounded and dead. Eventually, you find Comrade Difference Engine idling near the entryway to a small cathedral and you posit her your question.

"Insomuch as one can win a war, yes," she replies, "we won. The government has fallen, and the Aboveground has replaced it."

"You don't sound very happy."

"It's not over. All intentions and announcements aside, I'm not certain how long we'll be able to trust the new government. That's the thing about having gnomes in charge," she kicks the steps of the building, "about having anyone in charge."

She breathes deeply. "But it's over for now. For now, we're free. Tomorrow? We might be fighting again. Glad you stuck around."

"It's been my pleasure," you reply. "What now? I mean, this moment?"

"More than anything, I'd just like to return to our cramped little human room in the old Aboveground headquarters and sleep for a week. You?"

"Sounds good," you say.

"Alright then. I get the top bunk."

Your future uncertain, you walk through alleys and boule-vards and witness the birth of a new society on your way to a well-deserved rest.

When you get to the Aboveground headquarters, you grab the pneumatic canister—the one you took from the central ex-change—and pry off the top. A thin piece of paper comes out, with handwriting you can't read. Difference looks over your shoulder and translates:

"'Mother, I miss you around the house. I hope you get better soon! I can't wait until I can hug you!'" Difference puts the paper back into the canister. "It was addressed to the hospital, I guess," she says.

You think about the hospital, certainly overrun, and you look at your own bloodstained clothes. *No matter*, you think, because there is nothing else that you *can* think. What's done is done, and will never be changed. You can only hope it was for the best.

**The End**

### Acknowledgements

The first half of this book was written at **Pink House** in Portland and I owe a lot to **Ratchet** for her help. The rest of the book was composed during my stay at a writer-in-residency program at **The Cyberpunk Apocalypse** in Pittsburgh. I owe so much to the help and feedback of first readers, including (but not limited to): **Isis Grimalkin**, **Lyra**, **Kate Khatib**, **James Matthew Hoyle**, **Hugh Ryan**, **Stiv**, **Micah Gates**, and **Regina Zabo**. Thanks to **Flint** for the epigraph.